DISCARD

BLACK MOSES

BLACK MOSES

ALAIN MABANCKOU

Translated by Helen Stevenson

THE NEW PRESS

25 YEARS

NEW YORK
LONDON

Requests for permission to reproduce selections from this book
should be mailed to:
Permissions Department, The New Press, 120 Wall Street,
31st floor, New York, NY 10005.

Originally published in France as *Petit Piment* by Éditions du Seuil, Paris, in 2015
First published in Great Britain by Serpent's Tail,
an imprint of Profile Books Ltd, 2017
Published in the United States by The New Press, New York, 2017 Distributed by
Perseus Distribution

ISBN 978-1-62097-293-9 (hc)
ISBN 978-1-62097-294-6 (e-book)
CIP data is available

The New Press publishes books that promote and enrich public discussion and
understanding of the issues vital to our democracy and to a more equitable
world. These books are made possible by the enthusiasm of our readers; the
support of a committed group of donors, large and small; the collaboration of our
many partners in the independent media and the not-for-profit sector;
booksellers, who often hand-sell New Press books; librarians; and above all by
our authors.

www.thenewpress.com

Book design and composition by sue@lambledesign.demon.co.uk

Printed in the United States of America

2 4 6 8 10 9 7 5 3 1

Dedicated to all those wanderers of the Côte Sauvage who, during my stay in Pointe-Noire, told me pieces of their life story, and above all to 'Little Pepper', whose great wish was to be a character in fiction, since he'd had enough of being one in real life...

AM

Loango

I T ALL BEGAN WHEN I WAS a teenager, and came to wonder about the name I'd been given by Papa Moupelo, the priest at the orphanage in Loango: *Tokumisa Nzambe po Mose yamoyindo abotami namboka ya Bakoko*. A long name, which in Lingala means 'Thanks be to God, the black Moses is born on the earth of our ancestors', and is still inscribed on my birth certificate today...

Papa Moupelo was an unusual character, definitely one of those who made the greatest impression on me during the years I spent in the orphanage. A pocket-sized man, he wore Salamanders with thick heels – elevator heels, we called them – and loose flowing white boubous, supplied by the West African stallholders at the Grand Marché in Pointe-Noire. He ended up looking like a scarecrow in a field of maize, especially when crossing the central courtyard, with the wind shaking the filao trees that grew round the edge of the orphanage walls.

Every weekend we looked forward to his arrival and started cheering as soon as we caught sight of his old Renault 4L, with its engine that suffered, we liked to say, from chronic tuberculosis. The priest struggled to park his car in the yard, and would repeat the same manoeuvre maybe five or six times, though the worst driver in the world could have done it with his eyes shut. This grotesque battle was not simply his idea of fun: the aim, he explained, was that the front of the car should be 'pointing at the exit', to make it easier for him two hours later, when he wanted to drive back home to Diosso, ten kilometres from Loango…

Once we were all inside the premises assigned by the institution for his use, opposite the buildings we used for classrooms, we stood in a circle round him, and he handed out sheets of paper printed with the words for the song he was going to teach us. At that point the noise level usually rocketed, as we complained how difficult most of us found the arcane Lingala vocabulary taken from the books written by European missionaries, in which they had recorded our age-old beliefs, legends, tales and songs.

We concentrated hard, and within a quarter of an hour we felt confident, modulating our voices as Papa Moupelo suggested, the girls giving yelps of joy we called youyous, the boys responding as low as they could while he himself sat there with his eyes shut and a smile on his face, moving to the music, spreading his legs, then crossing them again. His movements were executed so quickly, we quite believed he was the fastest man on earth.

After a few minutes he'd be wiping his face with the back of his hand, panting with his mouth hanging open, and a look that said: 'Over to you now!'

And if we hesitated, the priest would leap in, instructing and demonstrating all at once. 'Come on now, don't be shy, children! Everyone join in! Jiggle your shoulders up and down now. That's it! Now, imagine your shoulders are wings and you're about to take flight! That's it! Now nod your heads at the same time, like over-excited little geckos! Marvellous, children! That's how you do the dance of the north in this country!'

Inflamed by these moments of jubilation, when it seemed

as though this servant of the Lord had come not to evangelise us, but to distract us from punishments we'd endured over the last few days, we'd go wild, perhaps sometimes a bit too much so, then realise we weren't really free to do as we pleased, we weren't in the famous court of King Mokoko, where the Batékés partied non-stop, while their sovereign snored, by day and by night, lulled by his storytellers' songs.

Papa Moupelo watched us out of the corner of his eye and intervened if we looked like overstepping the mark. There was no question, for example, of going up to the girls in the hope of grabbing them by the waist and fastening ourselves to them like leeches. He was equally intransigent with the more lecherous pupils, such as Boumba Moutaka, Nguékena Sonivé and Diambou Dibouri, who used bits of broken mirror to peep at the colour of the girls' underwear, then teased them about it later.

Papa Moupelo quickly called them to order:

'Now then children, I'll have none of that here! Sin often walks in with a smile!'

For a couple of hours or more we'd forget who or where we were. Our shouts of laughter rang out beyond the confines of the orphanage as Papa Moupelo entered one of his trances and imitated the frog leap from the famous dance of the Pygmics of Zaire, his own country! A dance quite unlike that of the northerners of our country, far more technical, requiring the suppleness of a cat, the speed of a squirrel being chased by a boa and above all a remarkable wriggle of the hips, at the end of which the priest would lower himself onto his haunches and do a little kangaroo hop, landing on his feet a metre away. Again, still shaking his hips, he'd raise his arms high in the air and give a great shout from the back of his throat, coming at last to a standstill, fixing us with his big red eyes. This was the moment when we'd give him a cheer, after which he'd adopt a less comical posture and we'd move to take our places on our bamboo seats that creaked at the slightest movement. We were all in seventh heaven, high on the mood of the moment, and we'd talk about it the next day in the canteen, or the library, the play area, the yard, especially in the dormitory, where we'd go over the moves until the six corridor wardens, jealous of this man of God's influence over us, would brandish their sticks and send us diving back under our sheets. We called them the 'corridor wardens' because that was where where they hid out, spying on us, reporting back upstairs to the Director, Dieudonné Ngoulmoumako. The most determined wardens were Mpassi, Moutété and Mvoumbi, who, as relatives of the Director on his mother's side, behaved like deputy directors, till Dieudonné Ngoulmoumako told them to knock it off. The three others, Mfoumbou Ngoulmoumako, Bissoulou Ngoulmoumako and Dongo-Dongo Ngoulmou-mako, who were proud of their family name, inherited from the paternal line of the Director, looked down their noses at everyone, even though they'd only got the job because of their uncle and had zero experience in educating children, who they treated no better than cattle.

As soon as they'd finished bullying us and left, one of us would say a funny word in Lingala, Papa Moupelo's language, and we'd leave our beds, form a little circle, and start our steps again, the steps that later would haunt even our dreams. Sometimes you'd hear the children humming the old-time tunes in their fretful sleep, singing in the old-fashioned language of this good-hearted man, who sold us Hope at the lowest possible price, so convinced was he that his mission in life was to save souls, every single soul in our institution…

*

Papa Moupelo had never admitted it was he who gave me the most kilometrically extended name in the entire orphanage of Loango, the entire town, in fact, and possibly the entire country. Maybe that was the way things were done back in Zaire, where they had names as long as they were unpronounceable, starting with the name of their own President, Mobutu Sese Seko Kuku Ngbendu Wa Za Banga, which meant 'the warrior who goes unstoppably from one victory to the next'.

Whenever I complained that so-and-so had not pronounced my name right, or had shortened it, Papa Moupelo would tell me to keep calm and say a prayer at bedtime, to thank the Almighty, because according to him, a person's destiny lay hidden in their name. To convince me, he took his own name as an example: 'Moupelo' meant 'priest' in Kikongo, and it was no coincidence that he'd become a messenger of God like his father before him. He loved the way my detractors called me simply 'Moses' or 'Mose'. Moses, he'd argue, to flatter me, wasn't just any old prophet. All the prophets, including the ones in the Old Testament that wore beards even longer and more grizzled than his, were midgets next to him: he was the one God chose to lead the children of Israel out of Egypt and into the Promised Land. Aged forty, revolted by the wretched daily existence of his people, Moses killed an Egyptian overseer who was punishing an Israelite. Afterwards he had to flee into the desert, where he became a shepherd and married one of the daughters of the priest who had taken him into his home. When he was eighty, and tending his father-in-law's sheep, God called to him from inside a bush and charged him with setting the Hebrew people free from slavery in Egypt. Did any of those who teased me have such a significant name?

Even as I write these lines, imprisoned in this place that was once so familiar, but is now so very different, I can almost hear the voice of Papa Moupelo, taking me aside to recite the biblical passage in which God appeared before Moses:

'The angel of the Lord appeared to him in a flame of fire from the midst of a bush. So he looked, and behold, the bush was burning with fire, but the bush was not consumed...'

I can picture him now, peering up at the sky, then looking at me for several seconds before saying, in his most serious voice:

'Oh yes, little Moses, the Angel of the Lord will appear to you too. Don't expect him to burst out of a bush, though, that's already been done, and God hates to do the same thing twice. He'll come out of your own body, and you may not recognise him, his appearance will revolt, even disgust you. But he'll have come to save you...'

During his next few visits, I stuck like a limpet to Papa Moupelo, so that some of the others started accusing me of brown-nosing, and being his midday shadow. All I did was beg him to let me sit at the back, in the very last row, remembering how he had enthralled us in previous lessons with the parable of the vine workers who turned up at the eleventh hour and got paid even before the other workers, who'd turned up at the third and the sixth hours.

'In the kingdom of heaven,' he had concluded, 'as for the workers in the vineyard, the last shall be first and the first shall be last. But don't panic: God doesn't forget little children, even if they aren't sitting at the back.'

No, I wasn't panicking; I'd been a bit worried, though, since I'd started expecting God to help me, especially when the Director beat us and no sign came from the Almighty to reassure us. I felt the Director was like the bad pharaoh in the Bible, who tormented the Hebrew people, and I wondered why God was taking so long to unleash terrible plagues on the orphanage, like the ones that forced the Egyptian monarch to acknowledge His superiority and His power. Or had God broken His word and chosen another Moses, a darker, handsomer, taller, cleverer, freer Moses, living in a different country where they prayed and danced and sang more than they did in ours?

My inner torment may have looked ridiculous and pathetic from the outside, but it encouraged me to read the scriptures very closely and find weaknesses which I could use to stand up to the priest, despite my great love for him. He'd be pleased to see me use the holy book to make sense of the world, even if my quest focussed mainly on my own identity and the meaning of my name. I couldn't use the book to catch Papa Moupelo out, he knew it like the back of his hand. And after all, I owed him respect: he was our moral compass, the spiritual father of all us children who'd never known their biological father, and whose only example of paternal authority came at best from the priest, and at worst from the Director of the orphanage. Papa Moupelo stood for tolerance, absolution and redemption, while Dieudonné Ngoulmoumako was the embodiment of malice and disrespect. The affection we showed our priest came from the bottom of our hearts, and we looked for nothing in return except the kindness in his eyes, which gave us strength, while the Director's sullen mien served only to remind us we were children to whom life's normal course had sadly been denied. The way that people looked at us said it all: to the Pontenegrins, 'orphanage' meant 'prison', and you went to prison for committing a serious offence, or maybe even a crime...

Of all the questions I asked myself during the period of inner turmoil that signalled the start of my adolescent crisis, one in particular haunted me day and night, and stopped me from swallowing my saliva, like having a fishbone in my throat: was I the only *Tokumisa Nzambe po Mose yamoyindo abotami namboka ya Bakoko* in the world? I felt positively about the length of my name and enjoyed the feeling of being a rather singular child. But Papa Moupelo also visited other orphanages in Pointe-Noire, in Tchimbamba and Ngoyo. I retained niggling doubts about the originality of my name. I was beset with jealousy even at the idea that I might be only one of hundreds, or even thousands of Moses, all of them better loved by Papa Moupelo than me.

Only he could reassure me. And since it was only the middle of the week, I was impatient for Saturday, so I could put the question directly to him. I did not, alas, foresee that an unexpected event would throw our lives in this forgotten corner of the Kouilou region into disarray. I could have foreseen anything short of an upset on that scale.

Curiously, and it was this that alarmed me most, Papa Moupelo didn't see it coming either, even though he was so very close to heaven...

BONAVENTURE KOKOLO, aged thirteen at the time like me, was beside himself:

'It's serious, Moses! Really serious!'

Irritated by him using my first name, Moses, I gave him a bit of a shove with my elbow and moved away a little. But I was forgetting that he was possessed of the obstinacy of a blood-sucking swamp leech:

'Where are you going, Moses? I'm telling you, this is serious!'

'You always say that – I know you!'

'Just look at the warders' faces – there's something they're not telling us! You might as well start weeping right now, I'm sure Papa Moupelo is dead!'

As a sob escaped him, I waved my fist at his face:

'If you cry I'll put this in your face, and you'll wake up over there, in the infirmary!'

'But he's dead! That's the end of catechism!'

'Right, so how did he die?'

'By accident! You'll see, they'll say he's gone to live with God and they've found us another Papa Moupelo!'

Bonaventure was my best friend. I was introverted by nature, and didn't show my feelings easily, but he was such a chatterbox they called him 'cotton bird', after the birds that brought balls of cotton back to the orphanage in their beaks to build their nests in the roof of our dormitory.

Whenever he opened his mouth, the other inmates all shouted:

'Shut up and go and eat cotton!'

He came back at me:

'The thing is, you're the only one who listens when I say things, the others are even worse than the Director! Have I ever lied in all my life? If I tell you something, it always happens!'

I didn't reply, and he looked me hard in the eye:

'That time I dreamed we were eating meat, we did, didn't we, in the canteen, two days later?'

'Yes, we did have meat two days later...'

'And when I dreamed the Director was ill, wasn't his eye all puffed up two days later?'

'Yes, he did it himself, walking into the door of his office...'

'So why do they call me Cotton Weaver when they can't even dream we're going to have meat or the Director's going to have a bull's eye?'

'You mean a black eye?'

'No, I meant what I said! Have you ever seen a black eye? Have you?'

'Bonaventure, you talk too much! If you don't shut up, I'll tell you to go and eat cotton as well!'

*

So that Saturday, as was our habit, dressed all in white, girls on one side, boys on the other, we stood in the main courtyard, on the look-out for Papa Moupelo. Today I had more reason to watch out for him than the other children, who were only thinking what a jolly time we were going to have in the catechism hut.

I really didn't want the priest to guess my intentions the moment he saw me. So I deliberately slowed down my breathing and murmured what I'd say when he took me to one side to remind me to pray and to thank the Lord. I had to be careful not to make eye contact with him before our one-to-one, or else, affected by his jovial, paternal manner, I'd defer till next week the vital question I'd never asked before.

While I was thinking about how to act with him, some of the boys killed time by imitating the noise of the tubercular engine of the priest's 4L, while others pretended to be parking, repeating the manoeuvre four or five times before yelling:

'That's perfect, the front of the car's already facing the exit!'

The girls, meanwhile, merely worked through the steps of the dance of the Zairian Pygmies, solemnly observing the taboos on their sex which we boys knew had been dreamed up at the dawn of time by men, to stop women discovering the little pleasures of life. For example, they were forbidden to eat boa meat, even though it was considered a delicacy in our country. If they ate it anyway, their breasts would drop to their ankles. Perhaps that was why the girls among us believed that if they sat behind the wheel of a car like Papa Moupelo's, they would sprout a little beard and their sexual organ would suddenly put on a growth spurt and turn into one like ours? At any rate, they distanced themselves from the boys playing at cars and discreetly held their fingers to their chest, as if the very act of looking for a few seconds at a boy pretending to drive a vehicle might bring them bad luck.

The warders that worried Bonaventure so much, Old Koukouba and Little Vimba, stood a little apart, engaging in secret talks of their own, a behaviour we had never previously observed in them. Old Koukouba was yelling at his young colleague:

'Stop pointing at the hut or they're going to guess what's happening and the Director will blame me!'

Suddenly a great nervousness whipped through the crowd. The warders stood to attention like soldiers. Bonaventure and I were the last to look over towards the main building where Dieudonné Ngoulmoumako had just appeared on the platform with the six supervisors, the severe expression on their faces contrasting with the more relaxed impression the Director was struggling to convey.

Dieudonné Ngoulmoumako was an old, fat, bald man of Bembé descent, a people known for settling the slightest disagreement with a knife, feeding children cat meat, and judging the wealth of any given person solely by the number of pigs he slaughtered during the New Year festival, weddings or periods of mourning. But which ethnic group did *not* stand accused of strange eating habits in that country? The Lari from the Pool region were known as caterpillar eaters; the Vili, on the other hand, from the Kouilou region, were coast dwellers and therefore said to be crazy for shark meat; the Tékés, present in several regions, were addicted to dog meat, while in the north of the country, a number of ethnic groups fed off the crocodile, even though they held the crocodile sacred.

'He shouldn't be smiling at us like that!' said Bonaventure, stifling his sobs behind me.

I turned to face him:

'If they beat us, I swear I'll beat you up later in the dormitory!'

'It's the Director – look at him! He's trying to be nice, so we don't cry when they tell us Papa Moupelo's dead! I want to start crying right now, not afterwards! I want to be the first to cry, because if I cry after the others how will they know I've been crying too?'

He was right up to a point: although the Director had for once put aside his dreadful beating stick, leaving the supervisors to do his dirty work, his apparent good humour didn't make him seem any more human. The tell-tale twitching in his right hand told you something was missing between those fingers, clawed and keen as an eagle's talons. Even when he plunged his hand into his pocket, pretending to scratch his thigh, he drew it out again almost at once, by reflex, and it dangled, ineffective and absurd, against his leg.

His presence on the platform was like a staged event of such mediocrity that the strings were visible the moment he communicated with the wardens opposite him with clumsy eye-winking, which we all could easily interpret.

The idiots playing at cars had stopped their little display and were trying to look like good little children, their eyes fixed, all the while, on the most feared man in the whole institution.

After maybe twelve minutes, the Director reverted to the man we knew and hated most in all the world: his face locked and bolted, jaws clamped tight, drooping moustache. He didn't usually persecute us at weekends, in case he got a sermon from Papa Moupelo, who once had told him that if he mistreated children he would have to answer for it one day on high, since those he was hurting were as like the Almighty as peas in a pod. What did we have to fear?

Dieudonné Ngoulmoumako was preparing to make an announcement, and so far, it looked as though Bonaventure was right. It was the first time our priest had been late by more than an hour and a half, almost half the time he was due to spend with us.

But even so, I was confident and refused to give up hope: Papa Moupelo would arrive any moment now, and would have his usual struggle to park in the main yard, as we stood by and applauded. He'd be wearing new robes, which he kept in a metal trunk, as he liked to tell us, to keep them safe from cockroaches and clothes moths.

'I like to look after my clothes! I keep them in my trunk, with a few moth balls on top, to stop the mites spoiling them...'

The odour of naphthalene mingled with that of our sweat. We never found a single clothes moth in our catechism rooms, probably thanks to this smell, which was ever present.

Yes, Papa Moupelo would be here any moment, and as though all this had just been one of Bonaventure's bad dreams, he'd hand out slips of paper bearing the words of old-fashioned songs, and we'd gather round him, clapping, and singing as loud as we could.

My illusions were swiftly curtailed when, with a solemn air, Dieudonné Ngoulmoumako began to walk towards Papa Moupelo's quarters, with the corridor wardens in pursuit. At a wink from his boss, Old Koukouba caught up with him, hammer in hand. Little Vimba was already inside, and emerged with a massive cardboard box, which he could scarcely shift.

Bonaventure found another way to annoy me: 'Moses, maybe that's Papa Moupelo's corpse, inside that big box!'

'Kokolo, don't call me Moses...'

'Why do you call me Kokolo, then? You know I don't like it.'

'See my fist? You want it in your face?'

We were too scared to go up to the box, even though we were dying with curiosity. Little Vimba was slitting it open with a Stanley knife, deliberately protracting the suspense.

'Why are you all hanging back like that? Come on, over here!' ordered the Director.

Inside the packaging we found red kerchiefs, and a plaque on which was written:

MEETING HUT FOR THE NATIONAL
MOVEMENT OF PIONEERS OF THE SOCIALIST
REVOLUTION OF CONGO

Horrified, Bonaventure whispered to me:

'That's the plaque they're going to put on Papa Moupelo's tomb!'

The Director was rapping out orders to his wardens, like some harassed master of ceremonies. He showed Little Vimba the spot where the sign should be fixed, so it would be visible as soon as you entered the orphanage. Then Vieux Koukouba was asked to hammer it up, since the Director insisted it should be the 'doyen' of his staff who had the privilege of putting it in place. This particular warden, who we secretly referred to as the 'Australopithecus', looked like an ancient chameleon, with his crooked back and eyes that pointed out left and right, without him moving his head.

But Old Koukouba couldn't get the nails in, and kept dropping them at his own feet. He leaned over to pick them up with clenched teeth, and we realised, seeing how much pain it caused him, that he had long since parted company with his cartilages.

Dieudonné Ngoulmoumako yelled at him:

'What the hell are you doing man?'

The old man apologised profusely:

'Boss, sir, it's the sun in my eyes. Instead of one nail, I see four or five, and I don't know which one to hit, but I hit it anyway. And another thing, these modern nails, they're smaller than the old ones we used to make coffins with, even the corpses never complained, because those nails...'

'Don't start in on the Pointe-Noire morgue again, we all know you used to work there! Don't worry, if you miss it, we'll send you right back!'

We didn't understand what the Director meant by this, but all of a sudden Old Koukouba straightened himself up and his eyes swivelled in their orbits as he focussed hard on hammering home the one nail he'd managed to pick up off the ground. He spat on the spot where he meant to plant it, and drew aim with the hammer held high above his head. Alas, again, he missed his mark...

Out of sheer frustration, Dieudonné Ngoulmoumako snatched the hammer from his hands, grabbed a nail himself and struck one mighty blow, the loud clang terrifying all three hundred and three of us orphans, and even the colony of cotton birds perched in the filao trees. After a dozen more blows, he stepped back, and looked with satisfaction at the plaque which was now nailed to the door of Papa Moupelo's room. He called the corridor wardens standing round him, and murmured something to them. The six men were falling over each other in their haste to hand out the red scarves and show us how to tie them round our necks. Each of us looked at our scarf, thinking it was similar to the flag these same wardens had fixed to the mast a month earlier, and which now fluttered in the middle of the yard, with a curious emblem on it: two green palm trees encircling a crossed hoe and yellow hammer, with a five pointed gold star above.

'So Moses, you still think Papa Moupelo isn't dead?'

'Shut it, Kokolo!'

Back on the platform again, still with his escort of wardens, Dieudonné Ngoulmoumako launched into grand-orator mode, explaining how we were the builders and protectors of the Scientific Socialist Revolution. On his jacket, just above 'where his heart beat', as some people put it, gleamed a badge with three letters on: CWP. You had to get up really close to read, in small writing under the letters: Congolese Workers' Party...

Halfway through his speech, which we applauded throughout, under pressure from the menacing looks of the wardens, the Director went out of his way to explain to us the significance of the emblems on the flag, which were also to be found on our kerchiefs. The red symbolised our country's struggle for independence during the 1960s; green was the colour of nature, so glorious, so bountiful, throughout our land; yellow, the wealth of our natural resources, pillaged and stolen by Europe, until our emancipation. The hoe and the hammer were there to exhort us to work, to engage in manual labour, while the yellow star was to remind us always to look ahead, to track down the enemies of the Revolution, including those living in our own country, with the same colour skin as ours, who were referred to as the 'local lackeys of imperialism'. In his view they were the most dangerous adversaries of all, blending in with the population, the better to undermine us from within. And in our orphanage there were already some local lackeys of imperialism.

His voice became more paternal, with the occasional catch in it:

'Yes, dear children, a new age is dawning, a liberating rainbow sent to us all the way from the Union of Soviet Socialist Republics! We will be answerable for the Congo of tomorrow and of the day after tomorrow if we don't settle our scores with those who for so long have trampled on our dignity, stamped on our gods, raped our most beautiful women, and imprisoned the most beautiful, the strongest and racially purest of our children. This new age belongs to you, my children, you must not allow the imperialists and their local lackeys to deter you from your goal. They know how to lull us to sleep, and strip us of all we possess. I will even go as far as to share with you the wise words of Jomo Kenyatta, the great militant and President of Kenya, our brotherland: When the *Whites arrived in Africa, we had land and they had the Bible. They taught us to pray with our eyes closed: when we opened them again, we found the Whites had the land and we had the Bible.* Also remember, dear children, the words of wisdom spoken by the President of our own Republic, for he too is a wise man, he too has a Jovian appetite for communicating and building bridges, lantern in hand, illuminating the dark labyrinth of our innermost hearts and minds. 'What is this Revolution?' I hear you cry. 'Yes indeed, what is it? The Revolution is something we create every day, by changing our old habits, and being vigilant in the face of the deviousness of Imperialism and its local lackeys. You'll find our President has made it quite clear: we must not get so carried away by Revolution and scientific socialism that we start believing they have magic powers. They are there simply to stimulate and guide our actions, not to act as lucky talismans. The development of our country, the development of every area of our lives in no way depends for its success on our being more-revolutionary-than-thou, but on our ability to act with patience, courage and good sense. Harmonious transformation, not fake transfiguration, revolution and progress, not depersonalisation, these should be our goals if we wish the Congolese Revolution, with its captivating youthful dynamism, to maintain that originality for which it has become a byword within the vast, unstoppable movement of world revolution, so incompatible with the slumber imposed on us by Religion until now...'

We listened to the Director with one ear, while the other was trained on the main entrance to the orphanage as we continued to wonder what had happened to our Papa Moupelo since the Director even avoided mentioning his name, as though he had never existed.

At the end of the speech, the applause went on for at least ten minutes, before the corridor wardens told us to disperse. Some, like Bonaventure and myself, went over to the library to do our homework for the next week. Others dashed off to the play area, behind the main building. The girls went back to their quarters where they were met by their governess, Makilia Mabé and her five colleagues, Marianne Konkosso, Justine Batalébé, Pierette Moukila, Célestine Bouanga and Henriette Mayalama, all of them Bembés, hired by Dieudonné Ngoulmoumako.

Our sleeping quarters were so huge that sometimes if you wanted to go over and have a word with another of the children you had to take really big strides, and there had never been as much noise as the evening they announced the Revolution. Our quarters comprised twenty numbered dormitories, each with ten beds, sometimes bunks, sometimes placed side by side with a small space between, as was the case for me and Bonaventure, so that it felt like living in a big, lively neighbourhood in which the smallest item of gossip would be picked over and analysed until late into the night.

Speculation over Papa Moupelo's absence spread from one end of the dormitory to the other, and led to lively discussion throughout all twenty dormitories. The priest had gone back to his native Zaire, they said, where the faithful believed he was a messenger from God, even though he didn't have a big grizzled beard like the prophets in the Bible. Overjoyed by his triumphant welcome, they said, he had built a church from okumé planks financed by the donations of the local population and the financial support of President Mobutu Sese Seko Kuku Ngbendu Wa Za Banga who, according to the same rumours, walked with a stick and wore a hat made from leopard skin when he wasn't busy throwing his opponents into the River Congo or having them shot and buried in a stadium. Across the water, the lame recovered the use of their limbs when Papa Moupelo cried, 'Take up your bed and walk!'; barren women brought forth twins while impotent men woke in the morning with their whatsit waving up above their navel. In short, Papa Moupelo had gone to a world that was more tolerant than ours and where he could do miracles which he couldn't here because the Director and his corridor wardens didn't believe. On this hopeful note we drifted off to sleep, some of us dreaming that Papa Moupelo was now dressed all in white, with wings on which he could fly up to paradise, while others like me thought he was already seated at the right hand of God.

*

When, over the following days, we passed Papa Moupelo's old rooms with hearts heavy from grief and regret, we pictured our orphaned shades still singing away inside, clapping their hands and dancing to the rhythm of the Pygmies of Zaire. Except we couldn't imagine the priest having much fun with them. The smell of naphthalene was stronger than ever, probably because it was buried deep inside us, or else because we couldn't think of Papa Moupelo without picturing his clothes packed away in an iron trunk and protected by the chemical that repelled or wiped out every kind of insect.

With every week that passed, the precious words we'd memorised with the help of our priest faded a little, along with the tunes of the songs that once gave us courage to face the week at school…

THE DIRECTOR HAD BEEN pulling strings to get his nephews Mfoumbou Ngoulmoumako, Bissoulou Ngoulmoumako and Dongo-Dongo Ngoulmoumako onto an ideological training course in Pointe-Noire so they could later become section leaders of the National Movement of Pioneers for our orphanage. They still remained under the control of their paternal uncle and particularly under that of two members of the USYC (Union of Socialist Youth of Congo), which was seen as the 'nursery' of the Congolese Workers' Party because it was within this organisation that the government identified the young people who would go on one day to occupy positions of political responsibility in our country. The Director's three nephews were thus promoted to a glorious future, which annoyed his three other nephews, on his mother's side, Mpassi, Moutété and Mvoumbi, who were still stuck in their jobs as corridor wardens, though they too dreamed of becoming the orphanage's section leaders of the National Movement of Pioneers. Unable to express their discontent to their uncle, they took it out on us instead. Their uncle had clearly favoured the paternal line over a family mix which might have calmed things down. Mpassi, Moutété and Mvoumbi felt they'd become underlings to the Director's other nephews and we revelled in the stormy atmosphere among the wardens, which sometimes looked like spilling over into violence, until the Director intervened and threatened to replace them with northerners – which was enough to bring them to their senses…

It does not fall to everyone to become a section leader of the Union of Socialist Youth of Congo. The government sifted through the applications carefully, taking account of the ethnic origin of the candidates. As the northerners were in power – in particular the Mbochis – the leaders of the USYC were also Mbochis, an ethnic group which represented a scant 3.5 per cent of the national population. In other words, Dieudonné Ngoulmoumako had had to fight to fix the appointment of his three nephews, who were not Mbochi from the north, but Bembé from the south. In fact he had only partly got what he wanted because although they accepted his request, the political leaders of the Kouilou region suggested he go halves: his nephews could be section leaders, but under the command of the two northerners, Oyo Ngoki and Mokélé Mbembé, who in turn would be accountable to the national division at the annual congress in Brazzaville, to be attended by the President of the Republic himself.

'Those two old northerners who come every week for consciousness-raising sessions, how come they're members of the Union of Youth, when they're not youthful and their hair is whiter than manioc flour?'

Bonaventure was always pushing me to the limit. It was true that Oyo Ngoki and Mokélé Mbembé were the kind of adult who looked as though they'd never been young, with their dark suits, and myopic glasses. Either they spoke to us as though we were two- or three-year-olds, or they used their own special language which one of them had picked up in Moscow, the other in Romania. Mfoumbou Ngoulmoumako, Bissoulou Ngoulmoumako and Dongo-Dongo Ngoulmoumako copied their way of speaking, using the same expressions, which they didn't understand and in which every sentence contained the word 'dialectic', or, as an adverb, 'dialectically':

'You need to consider the problem dialectically,' Bissoulou Ngoulmoumako would say.

'Dialectically speaking, our history has been written by the imperialists and their local lackeys, we must overthrow the system, the superstructure must not be allowed to outweigh the infrastructure,' Dongo-Dongo would affirm.

We never forgot, though, that before the Revolution the three former corridor wardens were just bruisers with zero intelligence. Now the Director had given them an office close to his on the first floor. They shut themselves in there to prepare *Pioneers Awake!*, a propaganda sheet that they posted on the wall of the hut of the National Movement of Pioneers every Monday morning. We had to read this publication before going in to class.

In fact all Mfoumbou Ngoulmoumako, Bissoulou Ngoulmoumako and Dongo-Dongo Ngoulmoumako did was reproduce extracts from speeches by the President of the Republic that were reported back to them by the northerners, Oyo Ngoki and Mokélé Mbembé. Each issue also contained a passionate editorial by the Director, addressed to the President of the Republic. Dieudonné Ngoulmoumako worked hard on it, believing that the Head of State would read it on a Monday morning before summoning his government to lavish praise on him. He'd announce in his weekly column that the President of the Republic was invincible and had been sent to us by our Bantu ancestors. The saga of his life was one of the most extraordinary ever told on the black continent: as a teenager he had captured a crocodile by the tail on the bank of the River Kouyou, struck it with his bare hand, stunned it and brought it home alive to his grandmother, Maman Bowoulé, so she could cook it and feed it to the entire village. While our future President was busy terrorising the entire population of crocodiles who no longer dared even leave the water and come up onto the bank to breathe on account of the presence of this exceptional boy, his playmates were struggling to catch palm rats in their parents' fields, or kill sparrows with catapults that couldn't have broken so much as a tsetse fly's foot. From which it can be seen that from a tender age our President was possessed of a sense of community spirit and a sense of sacrifice. He parleyed with mountain gorillas, protected elephants from poachers and spoke the language of the Pygmies, even though he had never actually learned it.

His second act of bravura was said to have taken place during the ethnic war between north and south, the former owing their victory to the intelligence of this precocious child, who advised the leader of his local combatants to dress up as an old lady and take him by the hand, as though he were her grandson. They crossed the line and arrived in the southerners' camp, where, by eliminating their leader, Ngutu Ya Mpangala, and his lieu-tenant, Nkodia Nkoutata, they provoked a stampede, followed by the humiliating discovery, the next day, that they had actually been defeated by a toothless old lady and her grandson, and that neither of them possessed a single firearm. This exploit, and the adolescent's intelligence in the art of war, so impressed the chief of Ombélé, the village where the prodigy lived, that he decided to send him to the military academy in Brazzaville. He was later posted to the Central African Republic, found himself in Cameroon with the rank of sergeant, and participated in the war being waged by the French against the Cameroons. When our country became independent, he was sent to Europe to complete his military training before returning to the fold with the rank of sub-lieutenant and all the aggression of a young wolf who wants to change everything as fast as possible. He had no time for the government he found in place, and therefore at the age of twenty-eight initiated the political upheaval which would carry him to power.

In his editorials, Dieudonné Ngoulmoumako underlined in bold that this was not a '*coup d'état*', as was reported in certain books written by Europeans, who were known to be frontline enemies of our Revolution, because we'd claimed our independence and when they'd been slow about granting it, had shed our own blood for our liberty. The President's mission was liberation, and he had fulfilled it with courage, and self-sacrifice. In creating the Congolese Workers' Party, the Union of Socialist Youth of Congo, and the National Movement of Pioneers, he was simply obeying the word of our ancestors, whispered to him in his sleep. The days when he'd covered endless kilometres on foot with a piece of manioc and a bit of smoked crocodile meat for sustenance were behind him now. According to Dieudonné Ngoulmoumako, the President was on a par with Jesus Christ, carrying on his shoulders all the sins of the Congolese people since the dawn of time…

I remember it was the first issue of *Pioneers Awake!* that confirmed that the government had decided to ban religion in all public institutions, including orphanages, with immediate effect, as the enemies of the Revolution were extremely keen to put a stop to our march towards the future. This same government decreed that the teaching of Marxism–Leninism should be our country's priority. When we struggled to understand how Papa Moupelo could possibly be an undesirable, since he had nothing to do with politics, the news sheet said that it was because he was one of the accomplices of the imperialists, that they often used priests to undermine our youthful scientific socialist Revolution. We don't know which, but one of Mfoumbou Ngoulmoumako, Bissoulou Ngoulmoumako or Dongo-Dongo Ngoulmoumako had drawn a crude caricature of our priest, showing him dressed as a magician from hell, hypnotising his audience, with the caption written in bold: *Religion is the opiate of the people.*

It was clear that Mfoumbou Ngoulmoumako, Bissoulou Ngoulmoumako and Dongo-Dongo Ngoulmoumako were incapable of running a news sheet which was so eloquent and intelligent in its expression. Most of the articles were thought up and written by Oyo Ngoki and Mokélé Mbembé, those two 'oldsters', who were probably also the ghost writers for Dieudonné Ngoulmoumako.

*

As for the hundred or so girls in the orphanage, they were put under the control of Madame Maboké, who spoke on behalf of the First Lady, President of the Revolutionary Union of Women in the Congo (RUWC).

The name of the President's wife was constantly on Mme Maboké's lips, and she would assure the girls that the First Lady was aware of their situation. On odd occasions she would arrive with an army of old mamas who would teach our young friends the rudiments of cooking with minuscule utensils which were supposedly appropriate to the age of the girls. Other times it was young girls who turned up to share with them the secrets of braiding and manicures. At these times the orphanage would be on the alert, and, in our separate dormitories, we'd rush to the window to catch a look at the 'gazelles from Pointe-Noire', as we called them, dressed in tight trousers and pointed heels, with their *pagne* pulled tight about them and their backsides popping like grains of corn in boiling palm oil. They'd wander about the yard and wave to us from a distance, until those bruisers Mpassi, Mvoumbi and Moutété appeared, objecting to these women from Pointe-Noire showing a kindly interest in us, when they scarcely even looked at them.

We longed to be little mice, and hide secretly in the girls' building and watch what the gazelles from Pointe-Noire taught them. In any case, our fellow inmates of the opposite gender were wreathed in smiles – perhaps to show us they were happier than we were – and we'd hear the echo of their laughter or applause, the cause of which wasn't clear, but which we joined in with anyway, from our own buildings, just to show them that we envied their happiness, and that we too would have liked to be girls like them, in these moments of delight.

Two hours later, the gazelles of Pointe-Noire crossed back over the yard, looking round for us, to thank us for having applauded even though we'd seen nothing, but we didn't dare brave the three corridor wardens, who were hiding out somewhere, not to watch us, but to get a sight of these lovely creatures' backsides. We would hear, with some sadness, the sound of an engine of a less tubercular variety than that of Papa Moupelo's vehicle: it was Madame Maboké's car. Not for one single moment had she taken her eyes off these young members of the Revolutionary Union of Women in the Congo, whose mission was to do the rounds of the orphanages, seeing to the proper education of our girls…

I N FACT, UNTIL THE YEAR the Revolution fell on us like a rainfall which even the most celebrated fetishers hadn't seen coming, I believed the orphanage at Loango was not an institution for minors who were parentless, or had been mistreated, or who had been born into a problem family, but rather a school for the very gifted. Bonaventure was more realistic, he said it was a place where they kept all the kids no one wanted, because if you love someone, if you want them, you take them out, go for walks with them, you don't shut them up in some old building, as if they were in captivity. He based this on his own experience, and on his own inability to understand how a mother such as his own, who was still alive, could leave him there, surrounded by all these other boys and girls, each with their own 'serious problem', which led inevitably to their admission to Loango.

In my mind, our studies at Loango were designed to make us superior to most other children in the Congo. This was the impression we got from Dieudonné Ngoulmoumako. He liked to boast that he was Director of one of those public establishments whose academic results were equal in every way to those of the state primaries, secondaries and *lycées*. He'd puff out his chest and declare proudly that the masters and teachers at Loango earned more than their colleagues at the Charles-Miningou primary, Roger-Kimangou secondary and even the Pauline-Kengué *lycée*, the most prestigious *lycée* in Pointe-Noire. He was careful not to admit that if these teachers were indeed better paid, it was no thanks to the charity of the President of the Republic. The running costs of the orphanage and the salaries of the staff were provided for by the descendants of the former kingdom of Loango, who wanted to show that their monarchy continued to exist, at least symbolically, through the generosity of its heirs. However, as I perceived it, our orphanage was separate from the rest of the Congo, in fact from the whole of the rest of the world. Since the school was in the hinterland, we knew nothing of the neighbouring agglomerations of Mabindou, Poumba, Loubou, Tchiyèndi, or our own economic capital, Pointe-Noire, which was spoken of as though it was the promised land Papa Moupelo used to talk to us about.

Yet the village of Loango was only about twenty kilometres from Pointe-Noire, and according to Monsieur Doukou Daka, our history teacher, it had once been the capital of the kingdom of Loango, founded in the 15th century by the ancestors of the Vili people and other southerners. It was here that their descendants had been taken into slavery. Monsieur Doukou Daka raged against the whites who had taken our strongest men, our most beautiful women, and piled them up in the ship's hold to make that dreadful voyage to the land of the Americas, where they were branded with irons, some had their legs amputated, some were left with only one arm, because they'd tried to run away, even though it would have been impossible to find the path back to their village.

Monsieur Doukou Daka would turn his back, lower his voice, and look out of the window, as though worried he might be overheard, then confide in us, in aggrieved tones, that many of the rich business people in Loango had been involved in the trafficking and had sent their sons to a region of France called

Brittany to study the secrets of the trade.

'You see,' he'd murmur. 'Sometimes we were sold by our own people, and if ever, one day, you meet a black American, remember, he could be a member of your family!'

He seemed to bear a grudge against the Vili, particularly since he himself was a Yombé, an ethnic group despised by the Vili, who considered it a tribe of barbarians from the Mayombe forest. The Vili and the Yombés, even though they were in the majority in the Kouilou region, each held the other responsible for the misfortunes of our ancestors.

We were shocked when, with his arms pressed to his sides, as though to emphasise his disappointment, Monsieur Doukou Daka shouted:

'What's more, the Vili took the people of my own ethnic group into slavery and sold them to neighbouring kingdoms! So don't come telling me that it was the white men who taught them about the bonds of slavery! White men still hadn't arrived at that point. End of story!'

Then, to lighten the atmosphere a little, since we were astounded to learn that blacks had sold blacks, he said we must wake up to the fact that we lived in a place that was drenched in History, that the former palace of the Vili King was less than two kilometres from the orphanage, at Diosso, and that it had been transformed into a museum, which some of us would be lucky enough to visit in years to come, providing we passed our intermediate General School Certificate.

Meanwhile, in the school yard, the corridor supervisors began to notice that most of the children talked constantly about Pointe-Noire, that magical and mysterious town, much praised by Monsieur Doukou Daka, who had been born there. In an attempt to remove any temptation we might feel to run away to this paradise on earth, they informed us that for our own good we had been separated from the children of the economic capital, and were being kept on an island, the most beautiful island in the world. If we escaped we would end up in the sea, devoured by the hungriest sharks in the Atlantic Ocean. The sharks were evil spirits, they told us, whose innate and fatal wickedness was stirred up by the sorcerers of Pointe-Noire. Why else would the bodies found on the Côte Sauvage be those of minors? The tragedy played out the same way every time: the victim-to-be came face to face with Mami Wata, half-woman, half-fish, who leapt up out of the sea, bare-breasted, with golden hair falling down about her shoulders and eyes as blue as the sky under the midday sun. The woman smiled at the child, opening wide her arms. As the child moved towards her, crying 'Maman! Maman!', she broke into laughter, its echo whipping up the waves to anger, so that suddenly they rose higher than the tallest apartment blocks, while the fish-woman abruptly transformed into a tough old shark, dragging the poor little sproglet down into the briny deep. The next day everyone would say it was Nzinga, the ancestress of the Kongo kingdom, who had taken the life of the hapless child, when in fact it was all the work of a few sorceresses from Pointe-Noire, wearing the mask of the one we were all descended from, so it looked as though she was to blame for the tragedy. The corridor supervisors exploited our fear and doubt, pointing out that when a kid vanished on the Côte Sauvage, people always said they'd been eaten by a shark sent by the ancestress, Nzinga, even if the body was discovered two days later, without a single scratch, spewed up and rejected by the sea.

Monsieur Doukou Daka laughed at these improbable stories

– why, he asked us, would our ancestress Nzinga send us down into the deep belly of the ocean when she was mother to all of us, and had given birth to the great kingdom of Kongo? Why would she set upon children, when she already had three of her own: the twins, N'vita and Mpaânzu a Nimi, and a daughter, Lukeni Lwa Nimi? If she hadn't had them, we'd never have had the Kongo people, and our country would never have existed, he concluded…

We were not surprised when Dieudonné Ngoulmoumako struck Monsieur Doukou Daka off the list of teachers at Loango, and sent him to his own town of Pointe-Noire, since he seemed so fond of it. The Director had explained to his staff, in a long letter, that our history teacher was an imposter who incited the children to run away from the orphanage and taught them to hate the Vili, putting it about that they had collaborated with the whites in the slave trade and that the blacks also sold other blacks. Since the Department of School Inspections and the regional department of Primary and Secondary School Teachers was run by Vili, it was not difficult for Dieudonné Ngoulmoumako to obtain the head of Monsieur Doukou Daka on a platter, and get him sent to a school in Mpaka, an outlying suburb of Pointe-Noire. Another history teacher, Monsieur Montoir, replaced him. He was white, and taught us mostly French history, featuring none of the characters Monsieur Doukou Daka had taught us about. There was no more kingdom of the Kongo, no more kingdom of Loango, and we heard no more about the Vili, the Téké, the Yombé, and even less about our ancestress, Nzinga, and her children N'vita Numi, Mpaânzu a Nimi and Lukeni Lwa Nimi. It was in fact the first time many of us had ever seen a white man close up; we'd always thought people of that colour were imperialists working with the local lackeys to put a spoke in the wheels of our Revolution. The Director understood our concern and told us one day in his daily address, before the raising of the flag, and in the presence of a blushing Monsieur Montoir:

'This white man is no imperialist, he is the exception that proves the rule, and at least what he teaches you will make you more intelligent than the little white children of France, because that imbecile Doukou Daka was an imposter, and I still wonder where he got his diploma from! Now, a nice round of applause for the white man!'

T HE DIRECTOR RECEIVED many visits from members of
the Congolese Workers' Party, and we were supposed to
set them an example. When these 'high-up people' were due to
visit, he became tetchy, yelling that if we acted like the kids from
Pointe-Noire we were so fascinated by, and showed no respect
for the national flag or the representatives of the Party, we would
receive a punishment we would never forget.

He prepared us for these visits, instructing us how to behave
before our guests. Of course there was no hope that these Party
members, who, unlike Papa Moupelo, were stiff and inhibited,
would get us dancing and singing in the club hut of the National
Movement of Pioneers. Since the men from the CWP didn't
speak Lingala, we wondered if they really understood what they
were saying in their French that was laced with adverbs and
present participles. Their vocabulary featured mostly difficult
words, which we called 'bad words'. *Anticonstitutionally* was
their favourite, and *intergovernmentalisation*, a word first used
by the Prime Minister, because up to that point each minister
had been used to working in his own little corner and the new
thing was to get them to talk to each other. On the other hand, it
was the Secretary of the Congolese Workers' Party, comrade Oba
Ambochi, who, as a put-down to the imperialists and their local
lackeys, maintained that they were constipated by the success of
our Revolution and were suffering from *coprastasophobia*.

We all lined up in front of the red flag and listened to these speeches, which were so mannered and puffed up that the next day some of us were afflicted with cephalalgia. As in the days of Papa Moupelo, when we talked in our sleep it was with the same convoluted words as the Party members. Except that now, even in dreams where the dreamer could lift mountains, leap across the Amazon or the River Congo or drink the entire Atlantic Ocean in a couple of minutes flat, he'd be incapable of reeling off the word *coprastasophobia…*

∗

We all wore wrist bands with our names on – I had to have one on each arm because my name was so long. We were put into groups of ten for 'community' jobs on Sundays, and since the President of the Republic declared the year the Revolution hit the orphanage the 'Year of the Tree', even planting a soursap tree himself at the entrance to the People's palace before the massed cameras of national television, we too, following Dieudonné Ngoulmoumako, had to plant a soursap tree, behind the central building, which made Bonaventure wonder:

'Is it the day of all trees, or just the soursap?'

'Kokolo!'

'You called me Kokolo again! Don't do it, I don't like it!'

Generally speaking, it was the children who hadn't recited the President's latest speech well enough who were made to sweep the yard. But Dieudonné Ngoulmoumako could decide to hand a broom to anyone who failed to lower their gaze before the staff or members of the Party. He shut up the recalcitrant ones in a building used by the Revolution, now simply used as a cell in which people were coerced into an understanding of the obligations of the pioneers of the socialist Revolution, with a heavy metal door and a small hole through which they slid rotten food. These 'prisoners of the Revolution' – as distinct from 'pioneers of the Revolution', who were altogether more decent, better-formatted, obedient – were forced to listen to the quavering voice of the President of the Republic on constant loop on a cassette player, supplied by the government to institutions like ours, which now reported to the ministry of Families and Childhood…

*

There were three hundred of us orphans, three hundred parrots, in fact, our heads stuffed full of things of no apparent value. That was all we had to do: learn by heart things which, so we were told, would be extremely useful for us boys once the first hairs began to sprout on our chins; and for the girls, once their breasts ripened like great papayas and their behinds drew the fascinated gaze of every man…

I'm quite sure it was fear of ending up prisoners of the Revolution that inspired us to recall with precision that our country lay straddled across the equator, that it had a total surface area of three hundred and forty-two thousand square kilometres, that the countries closest to us were Gabon, Angola, Cameroon, the Central African Republic and finally Zaire, with whom we shared the river Congo. Nor should we forget that before the arrival of the Spanish colonisers, and before we were turned into Christians, several of these neighbouring countries formed one vast territory, the kingdom of Kongo, and a certain brave and loyal woman by the name of Nzinga, mother to three children, two twin boys and a daughter, was our common ancestor.

When the Revolution came along I did a quick volte-face and was soon able to give fluent recitals of the speeches of the President of the Republic in our consciousness-raising classes. Visiting members of the Party congratulated me, which is why Dieudonné Ngoulmoumako put me in the front row and asked me to put my hand up to ask some question he'd prepared earlier, which was generally designed to reflect glowingly on him, and show how effectively he'd set us on the path of the Revolution.

I was unbeatable, particularly in my recitation of that memorable speech in which the President paid tribute to the workers, especially the women, of our country. As he put it:

'There they are, at break of day, with all their children, and even grandchildren. They transform nature, they create, they work in production. A few men are also engaged in similar tasks, and you are all, here, in our capital city, part of the poor peasant class, the most important in our society. It has become clear to me that there is a great difference between what I wish for and what I achieve, between what I say and what actually happens on the ground. It is clear to me that we run the risk of an ever-widening gap between directive and execution, theory and practice...'

His high-flown rhetoric meant nothing to us, nor did the Director's either, with his skilful intertwining of his own and the President's words. By now I knew how to flatter his ego. I simply recited his latest editorial from *Pioneers Awake!* and he was all smiles, nodding his head throughout and rewarding me afterwards with a Biro, which was an event in itself, considering he was as tight-fisted as they come.

SOMETIMES, I KNEW, Bonaventure pretended to be an idiot just to tease me and the other orphans. For example, he begged me to explain to him a lesson we'd had in class.

'D'you think Monsieur Ngoubili's right, when he says if you have two verbs together the second one must be in the infinitive?'

'That's right, that's the rule!' I replied, rather surprised by his question, since it was now a good ten days since we'd studied this in class.

'And what happens if you don't follow the rule?'

'Well then, people talk and write just as they please and don't understand each other.'

'Yes, but if there are four, or six or ten verbs in a row, what do you do then? Because Monsieur Ngoubili only talked about two verbs!'

'How are you going to get four or six or ten verbs all lined up together, as if they'd nothing better to do? When did you ever see that?'

At this he stroked his chin, with the air of someone deep in thought. I loved his very dark, unblemished skin, the dimple in his chin that got deeper when he was feeling happy. His face was thin and the bones showed through, but his body was good and strong, discouraging any other boy to give him trouble. But really he was just a colossus with feet of clay.

'Several verbs can come one after the other, for example, if you're doing ten things at once and…'

'Doing what, for instance?'

'Eating, drinking, peeing, sleeping, waking up, brushing your teeth, opening the window…'

'That's impossible, to do all that at once, you have to do one thing at a time, properly…'

'That was just an example, you're yelling at me now, just like the others, because you think you're cleverer than me! D'you want to thump me too? Shall I just lie down right here to make it easy for you?'

'No, I won't thump you, I've never thumped you, you know that! We're brothers, I'm not like the others, I won't play football with you one minute then turn on you the next…'

Unlike me, Bonaventure knew who his mother was. She would sometimes come to Loango, and though we hadn't seen her since the Revolution this didn't seem to bother her son much.

Zacharie Kokolo, his biological father, whose name he bore, had disappeared as soon as the pregnancy was announced. He was a public employee, working for the National Water and Electric Company. He used to fix the dials on the electricity and water meters at my friend's mother's house, so she had nothing to pay for years and years, or at least only a tiny sum which wouldn't buy you one packet of water at the Grand Marché in Pointe-Noire. He did fiddles like this on behalf of the entire population of the town, and the Pontenegrins paid him a sum of money in return. There was no risk as he was hand-in-glove with some high-up people in the Water and Electric Company. Bonaventure's mother would have been just another client, had Zacharie Kokolo not been determined to convince the poor woman he should take her as his second wife. He visited her

Fridays and Saturdays, in the early afternoon, and went home to his existing wife and four children around six in the evening, in Loandjili, on the other side of Pointe-Noire. Bonaventure's mother's other man was called Mbwa Mabé. The people of Voungou called him 'the official incumbent' and he often turned up three hours later after a long and exhausting day's work as a lorry driver in the Tchibamba district, on the Angolan border. He was known as 'the official incumbent' because he got in long before Zacharie Kokolo, the public employee, and no one ever really saw him, because of his profession.

So on the one hand there was Mbwa Mabé, a bachelor, childless, seeking neither marriage nor posterity of any kind, and who would disappear into the hinterland and come back a month or two later.

On the other there was Zacharie Kokolo, who had a good, secure position at the Water and Electric Company but who put off for forever and a day making any real commitment, that is to say publicly taking Bonaventure's mother as his second wife. And she knew full well that like many women in Pointe-Noire who had decided to be content with the small space allotted them by the married man in their lives, she would remain, for the rest of her life, the public employee's spare wheel, with no way of getting him to change his mind. Unless perhaps a child should result from this backroom relationship, in which the public employee, hoping to safeguard the reputation his illicit activities had somewhat eroded, still checked left and right before entering or leaving Bonaventure's mother's house. When she fell pregnant she was suddenly assailed by doubts. Judging by the dates of her cycle and the period of fertility, everything seemed to point to the public employee of the Water and Electric Company, since Mbwa Mabé had been absent from Pointe-

Noire for over sixty days, training the lorry drivers of a rich businessman who had just bought three Isuzu trucks. Zacharie Kokolo knew of the existence of the 'official incumbent', and when Bonaventure's mother explained that the other couldn't possibly be the child's father, he made no fuss, and seemed to take a pretty responsible attitude, along the lines of, 'Oh well, love, it was bound to happen one day, I don't know why people get so upset about these things. It's our child, I'll look after it like I do the others, don't you worry...'

Then, to Bonaventure's mother's great surprise, he dropped out of circulation. Perhaps he had realised that if he carried on seeing his mistress, the news would get round to his wife, who until now had always thought that even if her man was cheating on her, he wouldn't dare make a baby behind her back. Time and time again, Bonaventure's mother turned up outside the offices of the Water and Electric Company in the hope of seeing him there, and getting an explanation for his cowardice from his own lips. But she never got past the front desk. Every time she was told that the public employee was busy, that he'd be in touch.

Two months later, riled by his desertion, she returned to the front desk of the company and threatened to take him to a tribunal. Just as the security people were about to throw her out, she lifted her *pagne* and showed them her belly, which was already visibly rounder, though it was still early days. After this incident the company staff all noticed that Zacharie Kokolo decided to shift up a gear. He had influence, and he wanted it to be known. He began by using his connections to turn the game around and denounce his former mistress to the Water and Electric Company. In less than forty-eight hours the Company sent her bills for water and electricity going back several years, to be paid within sixty days. It then took her to court, two months before Bonaventure was born, claiming she was the one who'd fixed the water and electricity meters.

The courtroom was packed to the gills, as though it was a criminal trial. Most people were inhabitants of Vongou, who were not there to support the defendant, but to see how the judge was going to judge her offence, because many of them had also had their meters fixed by Zacharie Kokolo or other employees of the WEC who were no doubt also present in the chamber.

The National Company won their case. But in view of the condition of Bonaventure's mother, whose belly was on the point of exploding, the WEC declined to take it to the criminal court and merely placed a claim for the company's damages.

And so Bonaventure's mother went from bright light to darkest night; from light bulbs to a hurricane lamp and from water from the tap to water from the river, which she had to boil so it was safe to drink.

When her son was born, she decided to call him Bonaventure Kokolo, because deep down she'd always been in love with the public employee and thought it right and proper that the child should bear his father's name, whether present or absent, whether he liked it or not.

'The official incumbent' had broken off all contact with Bonaventure's mother and was travelling the length and breadth of the country at the wheel of the Isuzus belonging to the rich businessman who had at long last given him a proper job and a house in Tchimbamba, where perhaps he had married and was planning to have children.

After two months, during which the young mother was at her wits' end to know how she'd cope with Bonaventure on her own, one of her cousins mentioned the 'Bembé' who ran the orphanage at Loango, and said that if she went to see the boss and spoke to him in Bembé, even though she was Dondo herself, he'd grant her request.

When the young mother turned up with Bonaventure in her arms at the door of the institution, I had already been there a week myself, and we were both exactly two months old...

I could see why Bonaventure got cross when I called him Kokolo, but I wasn't sure what else I should call him, since that was the name his mother gave when she registered him and the name of his real male parent.

However hard I tried to call him 'Bonaventure', Kokolo was the name that slipped out. On good days – especially when we'd had beef and beans at the canteen – he didn't seem to mind. I could even see a glimmer of pride in his face, the pride in being the son of a public employee, even a cowardly one. On these occasions Bonaventure would boast that his father was rich, and owned land and houses in Pointe-Noire. Then suddenly his face would darken and the dimple in his chin would vanish. When that happened I knew he was about to explode with rage at the man who, as I'd often told him, could, with a simple click of the fingers, have taken him from the orphanage and transformed his life.

At this, pushing away his plate, he would paint a different picture altogether, of a cold man, a profiteer with a taste for young women. These words seemed to issue not from his mouth, but from that of his mother, who painted a darker picture every time she spoke to her son of his father. How else could Bonaventure know about the actions of someone he'd never seen, and who he believed to be the most selfish, most contemptuous, but also richest man on earth?

*

Our friendship was like the one between the lame and the blind man. He was my legs. I was his eyes, and sometimes the other way round. If ever I couldn't see him I looked for him everywhere. I started in the playground, went on to the store room, ending up at the place where we used to have catechism, where I'd find him sitting on the ground, nodding his head like a little lizard. He'd take a stick and draw an airplane in the dust, saying that one day it would land outside the orphanage, just for him. He was obsessed with planes, and the moment he heard one passing overhead, he'd leap up, run to the window and stay there till it vanished into the clouds.

Then he'd turn to me, despondent, and say:

'It didn't land here. They've forgotten me *again*.'

A S BONAVENTURE CONTINUED to ask me questions about Papa Moupelo, I made it clear to him that we'd have to get used to the situation some day, that in any case we had to pretend to go along with the Revolution, and learn the speeches of the President of the Republic, instead of the prayers and the dances of the northerners and the Pygmies of Zaire.

'I don't want their Revolution, I want Papa Moupelo back!' he'd grumble.

One afternoon, when we were in the playground, keeping well apart from the boys who were playing football, a sport neither of us was any good at, I found myself staring at him, perhaps more intently than usual, because I felt really sorry for him, and he seemed more affected than me by Papa Moupelo's absence.

'Is it serious?' he asked, in alarm.

'I was just thinking, you're lucky, at least you know your mother, and ...'

'Don't talk to me about her, Moses!'

Deep down, Bonaventure wasn't such a bad boy. He was probably a bit oversensitive, and had often hidden that side, though it might actually have corrected the negative view many people had of him. There was no reason he should be here with us in Loango and I was always wondering if his biological father might possibly turn up and take him away, even though he was thirteen now, and they would need to get to know each other and the father would have to find a way to make his excuses to his offspring.

Bonaventure Kokolo had arrived at Loango the same year as me, and because we had grown up together, and been cosseted by the same cleaning woman, Sabine Niangui, we had always sat together in lessons, as well as in catechism, when, if he was absent with a temperature or diarrhoea – the two things he suffered from most often – Papa Moupelo would express his concern to me, as though in the whole twenty dormitories that made up our sleeping quarters, out of the three hundred other boys, I was the only one who might have news of my small friend.

I would say that Bonaventure had gone to the infirmary, and was resting in bed, and Sabine Niangui was looking after him.

Reassured, Papa Moupeelo would joke, 'Well he'd better take his medicines then, I don't want him polluting the air with his diarrhoea!'

I don't know why I always felt I was much older than him, and had a duty to protect him, even to raise my voice to him when necessary. Maybe because he was a bit of a coward, since every time another pupil moved in to box against him, he'd fling himself down on the ground and shut his eyes, so as not to see their fists coming down on him. I would intervene on these occasions, to extract him from this humiliating position and remind him that at least once he must show the others he was capable of being mean and pretend to get nasty even with the toughest and roughest boys in the orphanage. He knew full well that his aggressors stopped their bullying whenever I turned up because they had not forgotten how I had taken my revenge on the twins, Songi-Songi and Tala-Tala, the big shots who had terrorised the entire twenty boarding rooms. They had had the dumb idea of pinching Bonaventure's mattress, and switching it with that of Songi-Songi, who'd spilled peanut butter mixed with palm oil all over it, and was afraid he'd get into trouble with the corridor wardens. Bonaventure went and told the Director everything, and the twins had the worst fifteen minutes of their lives, because they were beaten both by the caretaker, Petit Vimba, and by the wardens, Mpassi, Moutété and Mvoumbi, in the Director's study, which meant they'd done something serious. The twins waited a week, time for their misfortune to be forgotten by the other boarders, then went into action. They beat up Bonaventure in the playground in front of a dozen other boys, who were all yelling for joy, instead of calling for the corridor wardens. I waited a further week before smuggling some hot chilli powder into the refectory and avenging the honour of my friend without him knowing.

My bed and Bonaventure's were in dorm 4, with eight of our comrades, who were all sleeping like dormice the night I rose from my bed and tiptoed to dorm six to scatter the hot chilli powder onto the food that pair of gluttons left beside their bunk beds, to eat around midnight or one in the morning. I knew where they hid it, and it was easy to flatten myself on the floor just outside their block, extend my right arm, lift the lid on the plastic plate and sprinkle my hot chillies inside.

At two in the morning I pretended to sleep and was sniggering under the bedclothes as the two of them almost got into a fight over it.

'Was it you that spiked the food? There's so much chilli on there, I can't even taste my antelope meat!'

'It wasn't me, it was you!'

'No it wasn't, it was you!'

Before the first cock's crow or chirp of cotton-bird, the twins dashed off into the toilets, disturbing the whole orphanage. The next night was worst of all: they stayed in bed with dysentery, and the warden Mvoumbi, not Sabine Niangui, had to bring them medicines…

Attacking these two tough nuts was a daring undertaking, even if I had done it behind their backs. But I knew the boomerang would come back and hit me in the face. Songi-Songi and Tala-Tala weren't just anyone. Four years older than me, they had come from a little orphanage in Pointe-Noire, and been transferred to Loango in order, it was said, to receive an exemplary education so they could then be reintroduced into society. At our orphanage, instead of just waiting around for couples to come and adopt them, the twins would benefit from proper teaching. But they were uncooperative, constantly challenging the authority of the Director and the wardens, and not a day went by when they weren't punished or humiliated in front of everyone, like when they were tied up like dogs to the foot of a filao tree and left there even in the rain.

The Director would say, 'That will teach them life's no tarmacked path!'

He was referring to the tarmacked road that ran from Loango to Pointe-Noire, and which for him was synonymous with a nice smooth ride. In fact the Director incited us to hate these two young kids and encouraged us, without actually saying so, to thrash them at the least provocation. He had personally allowed the corridor wardens, in particular Mvoumbi and Mpassi, to put it about that the twins had been transferred to Loango after a fight during which they'd gouged out the eye of a boy who was older than them – but it was unclear which of them had actually done the gouging as the victim wasn't sure and the two brothers admitted their actions without revealing which of them had been responsible. The poor boy had owed them food, and I couldn't see how you could owe someone food, like you might owe money, or how it could take such a dramatic turn. Songi-Songi and Tala-Tala went even further, threatening their comrades' lives till they agreed to promise them their meals for the next day, and the day after that, so that some of them actually went without food for two or three days. Partly because of their size – they were at least two and a half heads taller than us – and partly because of their history of precocious banditry, they established themselves straight away as leaders of the dorms, and trained us in the ways of the kids of Pointe-Noire. They rummaged in the orphanage bins, retrieved cigarette stubs that had been dropped by the staff, especially the Director and the corridor wardens, who would throw down almost half an unsmoked cigarette, and straight away light another. We too had become little smokers, giving Songi-Songi and Tala-Tala food in exchange for dog-ends that got us so excited we'd laugh like hyenas. That was the first time I swallowed smoke, and I'd cough and feel like I was about to regurgitate my own lungs. It baffled me how the Director and the caretakers could like this drug, and consume it with no difficulty, while I felt like I was suffocating, like my thorax was on fire. The twins taught us how to act like grown-up people smoking; your head had to be a bit to one side, right eye half-closed, cigarette between your index and middle fingers, the end of the filter just balanced between your lips. You had to leave gaps between your puffs, and wave your arms around, as though deep in conversation with your friends.

I wasn't in fact permanently at war with the twins. On the contrary, they appreciated my ability to keep quiet, and deep

down they were confident I wouldn't denounce them to the
corridor wardens, unlike Bonaventure. And if they asked me to
recite the latest speech by the President of the Republic, so they
could learn it and avoid getting into trouble with the Director
again, I would do it just for them, to please them, in a monotone
voice, with my chin lifted high. This meant I could keep my food
or even get an extra ration, which they'd taken off another pupil.
This was my reward for not reacting when they laughed at me for
copying the Head of State, imitating his tics and stooping a little,
to be as small as he was. I didn't enjoy doing this, because it made
me look like a penguin, in my white shirt and short black trousers.
Having found their little game, and a star actor, they could just
point at me and off I'd go, though I didn't know why they laughed
so much when the words I was reciting were not in the least bit
funny. Standing stiff as a ramrod, I'd intone, implacably:

*'The President of the Republic and head of the Congolese
Workers' Party announced to the delegates of the federations of
the heads of the Congolese Confederations of Trades Unions: It's
irrelevant whether the leader comes from the north or the south.
No region is sufficient unto itself, no tribe can live in isolation.
The interdependence of tribes and regions will build a Congolese
nation which cannot be put asunder. Only national unity in work,
democracy and peace can assure our people certain victory over
imperialism and under-development...'*

*

I knew I could easily lose an eye over the business of scattering
the twins' food with chilli pepper. Even though I'd done it all for
him, Bonaventure felt so sorry for them that I no longer had an
easy conscience.

'Moses, it's serious, *very* serious! They're really ill, they're going to die! Someone's poisoned them and they've got even worse diarrhoea than I often get! We have to do something, I don't want them to die! It's not normal diarrhoea!'

In his head he had a list of possible culprits, and suspected the personnel of the institution, in particular the Director, who made no secret of his displeasure at having the two brothers in his orphanage, and would sometimes rant:

'They've sent me a pair of Siamese delinquents, because they know I'm very strict and will set them back on the right track, but they've already been badly educated elsewhere! They take my orphanage for some kind of penitentiary, and I end up with hoodlums like these! Those two don't belong here! They've brought their bad ways with them from Pointe-Noire to Loango!'

As soon as they were better, Tala-Tala confronted me on my way over to the showers:

'Pleased with yourself?' he asked.

'Should I be?'

'Aha, you think I didn't see, do you? You know what I mean! That's why you've got your head down! Look me in the eye and tell me you had nothing to do with our diarrhoea!'

Since I didn't look up he concluded, 'Every single thing you do, by day or by night, appears to me and my brother in a dream! Just because you were here first doesn't mean we have to respect you. And so what if Sabine Niangui protects you like she was your mother, we're going to teach her a lesson, so you don't do anything stupid again!'

'No, not Sabine, you leave her alone!'

'OK then, so why did you put those chillies in our food?'

'Bonaventure's not a bad boy, but ever since you got here he's been terrified, you beat him up in front of all the others, and he is a bit like my brother and...'

To my great surprise, he was rather conciliatory:

'Songi-Songi agrees with me, we'll let this one go, we'll lay off your little chicken-friend, but you have to make amends, because we had the worst time, for days and days...'

'Make amends? But I didn't do anything bad...'

'Moses, for now I'm being nice...'

'And besides, I...'

'Don't push me too hard, Moses... You know my brother, Songi-Songi, he's not going to be too happy when I tell him you refused to help us when we nearly died from your chilli peppers...'

As I was already well acquainted with Tala-Tala's character, I capitulated, with an image in my head of the machete he'd tried to smuggle into the orphanage. Mvoumbi, the caretaker, had seized the weapon, thanks to Louyindoula, who had spilled the beans. It would be an understatement to say that this particular pupil didn't care for them one bit, and his hatred went back a long way. Louyindoula had younger twin sisters himself, and when they were born he quickly realised his parents had eyes for no one but their two little fairy dolls. He went off and sulked alone, on fire with rage and jealousy, until one day they came across him, aged four, asphyxiating his two sisters while they slept. Four months later, he savagely bit the left big toe of one of the twins, and the thumb of the other. He had to be watched the whole time because with his big red eyes and microcephalous head he fitted the profile of the criminals spreading terror in the streets of Pointe-Noire. The father decided to put his name down for Loango orphanage, hoping that with time, growing up surrounded by other boys, he would learn to be more sociable and less jealous. Unfortunately, he arrived the same year as Songi-Songi and Tala-Tala, and these two boys reminded him of his own situation. The war between them in the dormitory was vicious on both sides, but the twins always came out on top.

Tala-Tala broke in on my thoughts.

'So, to cancel out what you did, you have to work for us…'

'What kind of work?'

'Louyindoula's pinched Monganga's soap and my brother's toothpaste. You have to go and find him and work out a way to bring him round to the back of the storehouse, where we can teach him a proper lesson, we've had enough, it's gone on too long…'

The twins already had well-developed muscles and a fine down on their upper lips. I often found it hard to tell one from the other. I had to peer at their faces closely to see that Songi-Songi – born a few minutes earlier – had a little black mark in the white of his right eye, and Tala-Tala had the same in the white of his left eye. Every time I got it the wrong way round, thinking that Songi-Songi's black mark was in his left eye and Tala-Tala's in his right eye, when in fact it was the other way round. And in any case, what was the use of telling them apart when they were constantly together and wore exactly the same clothes?

So it was for Bonaventure's sake that I took the risk of becoming the twins' accomplice in their campaign against Louyindoula. The only way they managed to corner him near the store at the far end of the main building was by me acting as bait, persuading Louyindoula to follow me to a place where I'd promised he'd see something amazing, something he'd never seen in his life before and which had to be kept a secret. Curious, he swore not to tell anyone and followed me at once. We arrived round the back of the store to find Songi-Songi and Tala-Tala already there, each with a piece of wood in his hands. They leapt on poor Louyindoula and beat him before my eyes, while I faked surprise at the ambush, so as not to attract the anger of the unfortunate victim, who was yelling for help, asking me to intervene and 'do something'. Alas his cries were drowned by the shouts coming from the play area, where a football match was taking place, watched by Old Koukouba and Little Vimba, with three corridor wardens acting as referees.

Louyindoula couldn't report the twins, or they'd take it out on him every day. He was aware, as we were, that since the discovery of the machete under Tala-Tala's bed, even the care-takers and wardens, and to some extent the Director, lived in fear of the two brothers. What had they intended to do with this implement – or rather, weapon? The Director explained that they were hatching a plot to escape like the one they'd seen in a film which, despite being underage, they'd seen in the cinema Rex, and in which a character had managed to escape from the prison on the island of Alcatraz, with the highest security in the whole of the United States. He and two accomplices had each dug a hole in their cell and managed to get away on an inflatable raft which they'd made themselves. The Director made it clear, however, that the twins had not brought the machete into the orphanage for digging with; they were planning, he said, to take a warden or caretaker hostage and threaten to cut his throat if anyone tried to stop them fleeing.

Louyindoula had been congratulated by the Director for reporting the twins to the wardens in the past, but this time Louyindoula had a black eye, and so when the wardens asked him who he'd been fighting with, the poor fellow swore in God's name that he had slipped on a bar of soap when taking a shower.

It was all because of Bonaventure that the twins now considered me their third man, so much so that people referred to us as the 'triplets'. So there were three of us, like the fugitives from the island of Alcatraz that the Director had spoken about.

Bonaventure was not at all happy, believing that Songi-Songi and Tala-Tala were stealing the only friend he could trust. I explained for the millionth time that the only reason I was close to the twins was so I could protect him, and that from now on the two brothers would stop hitting him...

I can still see myself lying on my back, with sores all round my mouth, and blocked up with a cold. The other children are all at school, the little ones in the two buildings behind the store house where we kept our work tools, the older ones in the building next to the refectory.

I sense a strange presence in the room, as though someone's playing at spying on me. Bonaventure often played this kind of trick, to frighten me. He'd hide somewhere, then suddenly leap into my bed, with a great cry, like a rabid beast. Sometimes he'd actually pull it off, and I'd be seized with fear, and yell for help at the top of my voice, provoking a disturbance in the neighbouring blocks, until we began to laugh about it.

I poke my head out from under my sheet, hoping to catch Bonaventure at his own game, despite my enfeebled state. In fact it's a pleasant surprise: it's Sabine Niangui. She's standing there with a glass of water in one hand and an aspirin in the other. My eyes take in the grey hair curling on the side of her head. She's short-sighted, and her huge glasses intimidate me, but I admire them too, and they make me think Niangui probably spent her youth reading books in even smaller print than the Bible, which, over time, destroyed her eyesight. Like her, I long to read and re-read books written in even smaller letters than the ones I read in the orphanage library, so what if they ruin my eyes and I end up wearing huge glasses like hers…

She's just placed a glass of water on the floor, and sat down on my bed. She says that with the departure of Papa Moupelo it's like a page of our orphanage's history has been torn out. She has tears in her eyes as she tells me:

'The Director could have kept him here, he never hurt anyone… Dieudonné Ngoulmoumako already humiliated me, years ago, by making me into the person you see today. If I'd had a choice, I'd have given up this job…'

She's silent for a moment, because she's just realised I don't understand what she means. She clears her throat, then continues: 'I don't know why I'm telling you all this today, when I should have told you years ago… I know you much better than you know me, and besides, do you really know me? I'm very touched that you've never been the slightest bit curious about my life. I suppose to you I'm just part of the furniture, a woman who's been there since you were born and who, you imagine, will be here for the rest of your life…'

She wipes away the mist that has clouded her glasses:

'I'll tell you this: I live all alone in a district on the outskirts of Pointe-Noire, not far from the Mongo-Kamba cemetery, ten kilometres from here. When I can't afford my fare, I leave home at four in the morning to get here in time for work. As I walk kilometre after kilometre, along the edge of the main road, with my eyes on the ground, I think about when I first got the job at the orphanage, which at the time was run by white religious people. Oh, those were the days, Moses, my little friend! Nothing at all like today, when the education of children's all mixed up with politics and orphanages are considered laboratories of the Revolution, it was better back then! I was young, beautiful, but was I happy? What is happiness? Do you know? Do you?'

I think to myself that for me happiness would be to wake up the next morning feeling well and say to her at last, 'Thank you', a phrase which till now has never crossed my lips…

'Back then, dear Moses, the children called me "Mama Organiser", and there were only thirty or so orphans, mostly girls, a good dozen of them abandoned by their parents because in their families, it was considered a failure to have a first child who was a girl. My job was to keep them amused, help them with their homework, or teach them songs in the main courtyard. There were only three buildings in the orphanage at that time, whereas now we have six, counting the room where the caretakers, Old Koukouba and Little Vimba, live, near the entrance, and the one behind the classrooms, which since the coming of the Revolution, you've called "prison". Most of our life was spent in the main building, with the religious people living above, while on the ground floor the canteen separated the girls' sleeping quarters from the boys', which were much larger but also harder to keep clean, because they had lots of windows and the dust came in from the playground. At night, little monkeys like you and Bonaventure crept into the refectory to steal bread, corn, or fruits laid out for breakfast the following day. Did that make Father Jurek Wilski, the Polish Director, angry? Oh, no, not him! At worst Father Wilski would instruct the kitchen staff to leave out some things to nibble, because he knew the children would be passing through. When the children could only express themselves in the local languages – which I still speak to this day – I would act as go-between for them with the religious staff. Back then I didn't have to walk huge distances to get to work, I lived here, in the room next to Papa Moupelo's, which is now just a cupboard where they keep cleaning fluids and equipment. I felt quite at home here, probably because I'd lived at the National Orphanage for Girls in Loandjili and, according to Marie-Adélaïde, who ran it, had been enrolled there by my own biological mother, a plucky woman who bought and sold things on the border between Pointe-Noire and Angola. What did she get from selling peanuts and bananas? Nothing, my friend, but she had to survive, and she said it was the only way to earn a living. She couldn't depend on my father, a Cuban soldier she'd met on the border, and who'd stopped to buy some roasted peanuts from her. He didn't just buy peanuts, he stayed longer, the whole night in fact, in a little whore-hut which one of their superiors rented close by for their weekend entertainment, if you get my drift...'

Suddenly serious, she adjusts her glasses: 'I am the fruit of that one-night encounter, during which my mother may have said nothing, since she spoke no Spanish, and my father kept silent too, as he spoke neither French nor any one of the dozens of languages of our country. My father, I'm told, was tall, handsome, with light brown eyes. I get my light skin from him; when I was young I was both teased and envied for it. People made fun of it because you could see straight away I wasn't as black as the Congolese girls, so I had to be a bastard, "a Cuban", which meant my mother must have gone with some soldier, either because she wanted to have a child who was less black, or because she was secretly working as a prostitute near the military camps on the border, but I favour the first possibility. Yes, she did want to have a child with lighter skin, because at the time that represented a kind of superiority, it was silly, but it was all part of the complex we had about white people, anything white was superior, everything black was doomed, with no future, no tomorrow, are you still with me, Moses my friend...?'

I look at her hard, and try to imagine this Cuban father of hers. I've never seen a Cuban in my life, and as I listen to her talking about this man I wonder if she admires or resents him.

'He was a good-looking man, my father, he came to Africa at the time his country intervened in Angola, when the situation there was one of the most troubled anywhere on our continent. You'd see Cuban soldiers everywhere in Pointe-Noire, and they held the same fascination for young women as the sailors who came ashore at the maritime port, from far-away countries, in their white uniforms, with bronzed skin and a desire to let off steam in the bars of the economic capital. For young women like my mother, these soldiers were their sailors, and over 5,000 of them arrived in Angola, on the orders of their President, Fidel Castro! Well, they had to amuse themselves somehow!'

She smiles, and at once she looks ten years younger.

'Seriously, Moses, the Cubans turned up in Angola to help their "Communist brothers" in the MPLA (the Popular Movement for the Liberation of Angola), led by Agostinho Neto, who was at war with UNITA (the National Union for Total Independence of Angola), led by Jonas Savimbi, supported by the United States, by the racist regime in South Africa and even our neighbours in Zaire! So the Cubans were our heroes, because our country openly supported Agostinho Neto's MPLA. On their days off, the soldiers would leave Angola and roam all over Pointe-Noire. Who could blame them for taking advantage of their prestige to satisfy the young girls who fell at their feet, even though they knew full well these encounters had no future? Every time I look at the island of Cuba on a map I remind myself that my father was born somewhere there, in Havana, or Santiago de Cuba, or Las Tunas, Bayamo, Pinar del Rio or Santa Clara, but to me they're just the names of cities, I don't feel any particular attachment to this distant country, I'm no different really to all those tourists who dream of beaches with fine sand, music at every crossroads, the bright colours of those American cars from the 1950s, or the Ladas and Moskvitches, imported from the Soviet Union, driven by men with fat cigars between their lips. When I was born my mother put me in the National Orphanage for Girls in Loandjili. A bit later I realised half the girls in there had a Cuban soldier for a father, as though the institution had actually been created especially for them, or as though the orphanage practised a kind of positive discrimination, accepting only girls of Congo–Cuban origin. Sure enough I discovered a bit later that the place was entirely funded by the Cuban president, Fidel Castro. My mother intended to take me back when she'd managed to sort herself out. But really, my friend, that's probably what most of the parents said, so they didn't have to feel guilty about cutting themselves off from their offspring. What do they say? "Never put off to tomorrow what you can do today?" My mother should have heeded that, because sadly, she died three years after I went into the orphanage, after an attack by bandits on the border, where she continued to ply her trade. The orphanage only heard about it two months later, the day a couple turned up to adopt me. The woman who was to become my adoptive mother was crazy about my putty-coloured skin, my big eyes and afro hair. In fact until I reached adolescence she refused to let me have braids and nicknamed me "Angela Davis', after a black American activist you may have heard of. I liked her calling me this, especially when I learned that this woman had fought for the freedom of black people in America and that she belonged to that brave organisation known as the Black Panthers. My new parents decided to call me simply by the pretty name of Angela, it was younger-sounding and more poetic than Sabine... Are you falling asleep?'

'No, I'm listening...'

'To be honest, I don't regret being adopted by this couple, as they sent me to a private school in the town centre, and after that I went to the private Pasteur secondary school, and on to the Victor Augagneur lycée, where I got my baccalaureate in literature and philosophy with top marks, even though I was one of the youngest students in the school. If I'd gone on to university in Brazzaville, where my parents intended to enrol me, perhaps I would have got a job in a high-up office, or been in charge of men and women who feared and respected me. But there you are, at seventeen I let a man touch me for the first time, then take away the innocence which till then had distinguished me from the young girls of Pointe-Noire whose future was prematurely ruined by thoughtless – I might say irresponsible – lovers. The man was forty, married, and worked as a postman in the National Office of Post and Telecommunications. I'd known him since I was three, and felt completely safe with him, perhaps because he'd watched me growing up, calling in on weekdays to drop off the post at my parents' house, chat for a few minutes with my father, accept a glass of palm wine from my mother. He'd hang around at our house, stroking my little afro mop, complimenting my parents: "When she gets older you must get her one of those haircuts you see on black American actresses in films at the Rex! I swear, she'll be a heartbreaker, this little princess!" Yes, my friend, this is the man who got me pregnant fourteen years later, you can imagine the scandal that erupted in our family, especially since he actually took my virginity in our family home. My father, who was careful of his reputation, was beside himself, while my mother tried to convince him that they should have seen it coming, even if it was too soon, and with the wrong person. Papa disagreed and threatened to throw me out of the house. As a last resort, my mother proposed a solution which, to her mind, would suit everyone: get rid of the shameful foetus, which would otherwise remind them for the rest of their lives of the ungrateful postman, who now avoided our house, and got one of his young colleagues to deliver my parents' mail…'

Once again she takes off her glasses and wipes them, even though there is no mist on them. It must be a reflex, a tic, and I think that when I get glasses I'll make sure I do that too.

'My dear Moses, I wasn't going to harm the fragile little being developing inside me. I could already picture its little Cuban head, its eyes, its little arms, its tears and smiles. I ate at all hours of the day, hoping it would help its development, and even bring its date of birth forward a little. It pained me to hear my parents talking about getting rid of it, booking an appointment for the following week in the surgery of a white doctor in the town centre. Yes, Moses, they wanted a white doctor to do it because they didn't trust the Congolese doctors who, so they said, told their patients' secrets in the bars of the run-down districts of Pointe-Noire. I asked myself so many questions: why had I been allowed to live when I too was the fruit of a one-night stand? Why should I not give the same chance to my baby, who hadn't asked for anything from anyone and whose only crime would have been to come into this world? My parents were out during the day, so twenty-four hours before the appointment with the white doctor, I packed a few things and went to live with two of my girlfriends from the lycée, Elima and Makila, in the Rex quarter, where they rented a house on Independence Avenue. These two friends showered me with encouragement and support. Makila began to buy clothes for the child. She got them in pink, as though convinced it would be a girl. Elima, on the other hand, bet it would be a boy, so she brought home little rompers and bonnets in blue. I enjoyed the independence I found with my friends. No more father shouting at me. No more mother keeping silent, afraid to raise her own voice in front of her husband. Did they try to find me? I don't think so, and I'm convinced this arrangement suited them very well. I was by now almost two months pregnant...'

She automatically touches her belly, as though she needs to check the child is still inside. Her voice changes, getting sadder and sadder:

'It was there, at Elima and Makila's house, that I noticed one day while taking a shower that the water trickling down my thighs was turning strangely red. I fainted at the very sight of the warm, heavy blood as though from some internal wound. When I came round again, I was out of the shower, Elima and Makila had put me to bed, and I saw, from their downcast expressions, that the baby, whom I had already nicknamed Chouchou, had decided to depart for the other world, in Mpemba, the land where the sun never rises and where no one wears a hat... Since the child, of sex unknown, had chosen this route, I myself turned to religion. I sang in the church choir of Saint-Jean-Bosco, where an old priest who liked me, and who I told my story to, found me a position helping out at the orphanage in Loango. So in fact, my dear Moses, I was here before Dieudonné Ngoulmoumako, who was a political appointment, made once the orphanage no longer depended on the religious community. They moved away to Cameroon, to set up another institution. Dieudonné Ngoulmoumako had used his connections to get this post, because he belonged to the Bembé ethnic group, the one which, being skilled in its handling of knives, had helped the regime in power to win the ethnic war against the northerners. During his first few days in the job, the Director began to shake things up and impose his own rules. There was no question now of me working with the children: he replaced me with one of his nieces. Since I was of northern origin, by my biological mother, and by my adoptive parents too, I was considered a descendant of the losers of the ethnic war, and in his eyes would remain an enemy, a sort of spy who would help the northerners recover the power they had lost because they didn't know how to handle a knife as the Bembés did. The Director was at my heels, morning till night. The entire canteen staff – four women and two men – had been sacked, replaced by Bembés and Lari and other southerners with no experience, who served the children dishes from their own region, like cat meat for the Bembés, caterpillars for the Lari, and even shark fish for the Vili. Old Koukouba was sitting pretty, he was a Bembé himself, and a few years later he brought along a younger colleague, Little Vimba, a first cousin of his. From then on the home was effectively run by a clan of Bembés, until the coup d'état which brought a northern president to power. Dieudonnné survived in his job, but only because he changes with the wind. Today he's one of the great defenders of the Revolution brought about by the northerners, whereas yesterday he fought against them on the side of the southerners. For everything you pay a price in this world, my friend. A moment will come when the wind will drop, and the weather cock can't turn, and will stand idle. That will be the end of everything, and I can feel it coming...'

*

It's break time. No one will dare come into the dorm, it's forbidden. Niangui's next revelation comes as a shock:

'Moses, you've grown up so fast, I can hardly believe it was me who found you, thirteen years ago, at the orphanage door, when I arrived for work. You were wrapped up in a white sheet, with your head poking out, you weren't crying, in fact your eyes were quite wide open for a child a few days old. I took you in my arms, and went straight to the Director's office. At first he yelled at me, as he always did when a mother came to him to ask for help from his establishment. I must admit that for a moment I expected him to tell me to get someone else to help with "my" child, but eventually he calmed down, gave you a quick glance, and sighed, "I hope at least it's a Bembé and not a northerner like you!" How could you tell the ethnic origin of a newborn baby, with no information about the parents? So it was that you entered this place under a cloud of suspicion, and, in the eyes of the Director, wrapped in his own paranoia, you had clearly been sent by the devil, with a secret mission to bring down the establishment under his charge. Worse still, he was convinced this baby had been left outside the orphanage by northerners. I personally couldn't understand why anyone would abandon a boy child. It was rather different from what happened in the Orphanage for Girls in Loandjili, where, as I told you, only girls got left at the door, because a proper family had to have a boy first. Thank God, the Director didn't throw you back out, but told the caretaker and corridor wardens to keep a very close eye on you, even at night, because he thought that around midnight or one in the morning you slipped out of your baby skin and turned into a northern giant, with a great big beard, like a member of the Resistance. That Saturday you were presented to Papa Moupelo, who performed a special mass. That was the day he gave you the name *Tokumisa Nzambe po Mose yamoyindo abotami namboka ya Bakoko*. And since it was too long and no one could say the whole thing, we all just called you Moses.

THE IMAGE I HAVE, when I think of Sabine Niangui now, is of the woman who helped me whenever things went wrong, perhaps because she felt in some way responsible for my fate, having 'rescued' me at the orphanage door. Between the ages of seven and ten, when the Director used to take his lash to me, and I'd struggle like a demon, I'd see a woman with a troubled face standing a few feet from him, watching the scene, and that was Sabine Niangui. You could tell by the look on her face that she disapproved of the methods of Dieudonné Ngoulmoumako, who, in spite of the blessed name given me by Papa Moupelo, persisted in believing I was the spawn of the devil, and that I used my intelligence to organise most of the monkey business that took place in the boys' dorm, or in the canteen, when the inmates started throwing chunks of manioc at the girls.

Sabine Niangui, who we simply called 'Niangui', gritted her teeth so visibly each time the whip made contact, it felt as though she was suffering on my behalf. She was forty years old, but to us she seemed like someone out of a different age altogether, perhaps the reincarnation of our ancestor Nzinga, except that Niangui hadn't brought two twin boys and a daughter into the world.

As soon as the Director had left the dorm, she would take me by the arm and we'd shut ourselves up in the toilets, where I'd take off my shirt. At the sight of the broad weals on my back she'd run to fetch some antiseptic.

A few minutes later, I felt her warm hands on my skin, and the cold, red liquid sinking into the wounds, as she reassured me in her softest voice:

'I won't put any alcohol on, or they'll hear you scream from here to Pointe-Noire...'

I kept my eyes fixed on her, thinking how lucky I was to receive this special treatment from her. But Niangui didn't just nurse me better. On many occasions she gave me sandals, shirts, pants, shorts, colouring pencils, children's books telling of dwarves and a beautiful princess, or others in which I devoured the stories of two girls who lived on a farm with animals who could talk, and conspired against humans.

The only presents I remember ever getting were the ones she gave me. The staff were forbidden to show any generosity to any one of us. Niangui was given some leeway, because along with Old Koukouba she was one of the oldest members of staff. Either that or, if rumour was correct, there was something between her and the Director which meant he allowed these gifts, and didn't sack her. It was said that Dieudonné loved women, and schemed with the mothers of our little comrades, Yaka Diapeta and Kiminou Knzonzi, and those of Nani Telamio, Wakwenda Kuhata and Kabwo Batélé. As they were single mothers, and thought that if they offered their bodies to the Director he would give their children special treatment, he was able to exploit his position to make them stay longer in his office, two or three hours longer, maybe, and when they came out, their hair was messed up and they had their *pagne*s on inside out.

I didn't dare picture the Director pumping away on top of Niangui. Dieudonné Ngoulmoumako would find it tricky, with his paunch belly, that flopped down as far as his genitals, and

even in the dorm we'd hear him huffing like a buffalo. He'd expire from a heart attack while squirming away like a catfish on top of poor Niangui, and I'd never be able to look at her the same way again, because she'd never admitted what was going on between her and him, when she was my shield, an unfailing presence, always there just when she was needed, constantly with me, since the moment I'd first arrived, and prepared to do whatever it took to protect me. How could she pleasure this dreadful man, who inspired such fear in us? I stopped myself asking her. I dreaded getting an answer that made me feel even more sad. The older boarders often told us that when two people make love they end up thinking the same thoughts and swearing to look out for each other. Which, to my mind, meant Niangui had gone over to the side of those who gave us such a hard time. I didn't want her to look after me now, didn't want her hands on me. At night, before I went to sleep, I'd shake my fist at Bonaventure, to make him stop bombarding me with questions, I spread out the mosquito net and hid under my sheet, and began a long prayer in which, instead of thanking the Almighty for giving me the name *Tokumisa Nzambe po Mose yamoyindo abotami namboka ya Bokoko*, I begged Him to put a curse on the Director and Niangui.

If only Niangui had spoken to me earlier in the way she did on the day of my thirteenth birthday, when I was in bed, I'd have judged her less hastily than the other boarders and I'd have known that the things that were said about her were a pack of lies…

*

The day after Niangui told me all this, my fever completely vanished, as if by magic. My nose was unblocked, my breathing

eased, and I just had a few spots left, though I'd disinfected them with Monganga before I went to sleep.

I was waiting for her to show up again, to hand me a glass of water and a pill, and sit down on my bed and talk to me in her sing-song accent that she exaggerated, probably to irritate the Director, who was known for his visceral loathing of all northerners. I'd apologise to her for having believed, like the other inmates, that she'd been carrying on with Dieudonné Ngoulmoumako. I was sure she would say: 'Don't worry, lies will never hurt me...'

For almost an hour I'd hear again her warm, reassuring voice. I'd feel her look at me fondly while I examined the grey hairs on her temples. And maybe I'd ask her to let me try her glasses, which still intrigued me. She wouldn't refuse, I knew. And all at once I'd see the world as she saw it, and everything little would suddenly look big when seen through her glasses, and perhaps that was how she spotted the faults of humans and could separate the bad ones from the good.

*

Niangui did not come and give me a glass of water and a pill. Something told me she'd never come back, that maybe she'd only told me all these details about her life because she knew she wouldn't see me again, and that, as she'd said, a page of the orphanage had been torn out, and the first sign had been the humiliation of Papa Moupelo.

Our last meeting began to seem more and more like a final farewell. After two weeks of no news from her, the entire staff acted as though she'd never existed, and no one even mentioned her name.

At that point I knew it was the end of an era...

I was wrong, though, because one afternoon, when I was on my way to the toilets, dragging my feet, my arms flat against my side, I noticed the shape of a woman a few metres in front of me, with a mop in one hand and a bucket in the other. All that was missing was the presence of the Director for me to feel nothing had changed, it was all an illusion, Niangui hadn't disappeared at all.

I wanted to cry out 'Maman!' to welcome her, but my voice wouldn't come out. I wouldn't ask her to explain where she'd been all this time. What mattered was that she hadn't abandoned me. That she'd come back, just to see me, why else would she have chosen that exact moment to cross my path in secret as I walked to the toilets? I was filled with a joy so intense that I could hear my own heart beating against my chest. I went towards her with my arms wide open, a huge smile on my face. She didn't move, indifferent, almost, to my excitement, her face rounder than it used to be, with small eyes, that gave her a look of perpetual gaiety. Her skin was darker than before, and just as I was about to fold her in my arms, she pushed me away with a violence I'd never known in her.

Surprised by this, I raised my head and suddenly realised it wasn't Niangui standing there. It was Evangelista, the young woman who was rumoured to have replaced Niangui.

'When's Niangui coming back?'

It was almost as though she'd been expecting the question.

'She's not coming back, not ever, she's retired!'

She told me, with a smile I couldn't decipher, that Niangui was too old, in any case, she claimed she was forty, but in fact you could add another twenty years to that.

Evangelista looked very cheerful. She'd only come to taunt me, because she turned straight around and went back towards the girls' block. I just stood there in the corridor, watching her walk away, and the further she got, the more it felt like it was Niangui disappearing, and that she'd gone into Evangelista's body to force her to tell me once and for all that she wouldn't be back, that the page telling the story of her time in the orphanage had just been torn out too, that first I'd lost Papa Moupelo and now I'd lost her too, the woman who was almost like the mother I might have wished for…

WE HAD NEVER SEEN the Director in such a state. He came pelting into the courtyard, and bumped into Kokela, the gardener:

'Well? Did you see them, the guys I told you about?'

The gardener shook his head, then the Director himself headed for the main door of the orphanage, peeped his head out, and gave a sigh of relief:

'I don't think they'll come today, it's already midday, phew, what a relief...'

Dieudonné Ngoulmoumako hadn't slept properly for months. Four men, dressed in black suits and red ties, had turned up unannounced at the orphanage and shut themselves up in his office with him. Things got heated, and we could hear the Director shouting:

'Do you know who you're talking to? I'll have you thrown out, or my name's not Dieudonné Ngoulmoumako!'

Even as the visitors were leaving, the Director knew they'd be back again, but when? He began spending less and less time in his office and apartment. To shake off his unwanted visitors he had fixed up a little room for himself in the girls' block, and every day before going to sit in it with the doors and windows closed, he'd issue the same orders:

'If those shit-stirrers come back, tell them I'm not here, I've taken a trip to Pointe-Noire for a congress of our division of the

Congolese Workers' Party.'

He became more and more ridiculous in the eyes of our fellow pupils, who couldn't understand how four men in suits could upset him like this when he had so much power. And when he finally decided to return to his office, in the belief that the four 'invaders' had given up and gone away, the Director was surprised to see them back again, as though they'd been hiding out with binoculars opposite the orphanage, just waiting for this moment.

Dieudonné Ngoulmoumako had had enough. He called everyone together in the yard and standing on the platform, with his six caretakers behind him, announced:

'We are going to throw out these invaders who've come nitpicking in my tonsure! And the only way to do it is to get our voices heard right at the pinnacle of the Republic, because I'm quite sure the President is unaware of this witch hunt against me. We're going to go on hunger strike, until the Minister for Families and Childhood asks these people to go away and leave me alone.'

A few days before this, however, in an editorial in *Pioneers Awake!*, the Director congratulated the Minister for Families and Childhood on his nomination of new heads of public – and indeed private – establishments for the care of minors who were not just orphans.

The Director painted a rather flattering picture of the new minister, Rex Kazadi:

'Gifted with the intelligence and wisdom which gained him a place among the most brilliant graduates of the Ecole Nationale d'Administration, Rex Kazadi embodies the awakening of our

nation, the new face of a policy which is both rigorous and – more than ever – dedicated to the service of the people. This young man was known in Europe as one of those opposed to our country being taken hostage by the imperialists and their local lackeys. Rex Kazadi had managed to mobilise the majority of our young compatriots, and alert them to the dangers threatening our beloved and beautiful country. We wish him every success in the new role assigned to him by the President of the Republic, as Family and Childhood are the foundation, I should say the very cornerstone, of our society...'

In the rest of his editorial, the Director tried to defend his own house, but his justifications produced the opposite effect, and revealed that he had actually transformed the institution into an orphanage for correction – and protection – which was why terrible children like the twins Songi-Songi and Tala-Tala got sent there.

*

His speech was less enthusiastic than the one he had made announcing that the Revolution was entering the orphanage. He looked shifty, his voice was hoarse, his gestures were limp.

Even so, he found the strength to shout:

'Let's revolt! These northerners turn up here unannounced! What do they think this is, the Court of King Pétaud, all chiefs and no Indians?'

He could sense that this time things were different. He had omitted to point out in his editorial that the government was now inveighing against 'the bad habits of the Administration' and had actually created 'the Ministry for the Struggle against Tribalism and Nepotism at All Levels'.

'Yes, we must unite as one man...'

Looking across at the female staff he corrected himself...

'What I meant to say was, let us unite as one man and one woman, but my mouth ran ahead of my thoughts...'

In the face of general indifference, he struck what he guessed would be their most sensitive nerve:

'Do you understand the gravity of this situation? If I stop being Director of this institution, it will be mayhem, chaos, the end of the world, utter darkness, and you'll all lose your jobs as well!'

We all wanted to burst out laughing, but we felt sorry for him too. My real feeling was that his time was up, and that the wrath of God, to whom I'd cried out and who had struck fear into the Pharaoh of Egypt, the *bête noire* of the Hebrews, was on the march. This man here was just an emperor with no clothes, encountering the first obstacle to threaten his career. Instead of putting up a fight he had one knee on the ground and was shamelessly begging for help from us, who'd been less than nothing up till now.

And Bonaventure kept saying:

'This is serious Moses, really serious! He'll go to prison. He'll be in handcuffs, I swear!'

Gone were the days when Dieudonné Ngoulmoumako always managed to be in the right place at the right time, and switch sides in the blink of an eye. A product of the National Civil Service School of Brazzaville, he'd never married and never had children, which would, he believed, have impeded his upward progress. His Bembé descent was a sure string he could pull every time he wanted to secure a post in the administration. In this way he got into the office of the Minister for Public Affairs, also a Bembé, and then was appointed deputy prefect of Mouyondzi, the symbolic hometown of his ethnic group, where he stood in the municipal elections, but was beaten by a candidate parachuted in by the government. This candidate had not run a campaign and wasn't even a Bembé, but a northerner, who'd been at *lycée* with the President of the Republic. As consolation, he was appointed prefect of Mabombo, a town in Bouenza, his native region, where, three years later, he ran for deputy. This time too he was beaten by a candidate supported by the government, none other than the daughter of the President of the Republic's medicine man. The name of this woman only appeared on the electoral lists twenty-four hours before the vote...

Dieudonné Ngoulmoumako decided he needed a job that no one else was likely to want. When, as a consolation prize, he was offered the post of Director of the Loango orphanage, he hesitated briefly.

'I don't like children! I haven't got any, I don't plan to have any! Why can't I run the port of Pointe-Noire?'

He was given to understand that the port of Pointe-Noire wasn't that easy to run. It changed directors almost every year and he'd find himself sitting on an ejector seat. When he was assured that in Loango he'd be able to decide on his own salary, his own staff, and his own budget, and the government would have no say, as the money would come from the wealthy heirs of the kingdom of Loango, Dieudonné Ngoulmoumako finally agreed. And for more than three decades everyone left him alone and he was able to do just as he pleased, until the arrival of the men in suits who kept him awake at night, and seemed to be saying that the end of his reign was nigh.

As soon as the men he referred to as 'intruders' turned up, the

Director knew that he would be spending hours and hours in their company, answering the same questions a thousand times over. They opened boxes of files and whole colonies of cockroaches marched out, his office was such a dump, smelling permanently of musty tobacco.

He had to account for how we spent our time at school, and in the playground, our activities, whether there was any sexual interference with the children on the part of the staff, how often we were given food, and above all our physical and intellectual progress.

All Dieudonné Ngoulmoumako could reply was:

'What ridiculous questions! Everything's normal here! You really must stop imagining orphanages are full of paedophiles! They have that in Europe, not here!'

Without even being asked the question, he volunteered:

'Smacking a child is standard! That's how I was raised, and it worked! Let's not make a dish of pork and plantains out of it!'

Although he managed to make his case, and none of the children questioned actually reported any sexual abuse, he couldn't stonewall the inspectors when it came to his salary or his staff's, or the administrative jobs or the financial management. Why, for instance, was the purchase of a clock recorded under 'Hygiene and upkeep of buildings?' And how come his salary went up by over fifty per cent each year, while an old hand like Old Koukouba hadn't had a raise in over seventeen years? What were the reasons for the abrupt dismissal, without compensation, of certain employees like the carpenter, Bounda Na Gwaka, the stock-keeper, Mayele Nasima, and the cleaning woman, Sabine Niangui, who had all been hired back when the orphanage had been run by a religious community?

'I'm the Director, I hire and fire who I choose!'

'And thanks to this discretionary power, you've hired six wardens who are direct members of your own family?' said one of the inspectors, ironically.

'It was all perfectly legal!'

Dieudonné Ngoulmoumako had tried to insist on his status as supporter and member of the Congolese Workers' Party, thinking this would earn him immunity. The inspectors reminded him that members of the Party had to set an example and that from now on, until such time as his fate was decided by the Ministry for Family and Childhood – dismissal or relocation to a post in the backwoods – his three nephews, Mfoumbou Ngoulmoumako, Bissoulou Ngoulmoumako and Dongo-Dongo Ngoulmoumako, were relieved of their functions as heads of the department of the Union of Young Congolese Socialists within the orphanage. They became corridor wardens again, like Mpassi, Moutété and Mvoumbi…

∗

We'd been on hunger strike for two days, but the inspectors didn't show up. We'd had enough, and at night, in the dorm, we binged on supplies stolen from the refectory by the twins. What was the point of going on hunger strike if the President of the Republic didn't even know about it? On the third day everyone just ate their fill.

A week later, there were still no inspectors, but Dieudonné Ngoulmoumako organised a protest on the first floor, with his nephews. If the inspectors did show up, they would be met with a fine surprise. It was perhaps the only way, he said to himself, to make sure the President of the Republic got to hear what was happening to us.

OLD KOUKOUBA NOW HAD some serious health problems, and was rarely ever seen in the main yard. He had diffi- culty urinating, and when he did finally manage to squeeze out a few drops, he yelled so loud it was more like someone was slitting the throat of a bull in the staff toilets. A succession of doctors from Pointe-Noire attended him, all bald and wearing the kind of large spectacles you see on people who've studied in France, not in the USSR, but none of them managed to cure his urinary infection. They threw in the towel, claimed the care- taker's illness was linked to his senility and that at seventy-two his goose was well and truly cooked.

Bonaventure, always inclined to alarmism, foresaw a gloomy outcome for the poor old man: 'Yesterday I saw an old crow perched on the roof of the caretakers' hut, and it was looking at me so strangely, I was about to ask him what his problem was, but suddenly he flew away! How weird is that? He must have been trying to tell me Old Koukouba was going to die soon, don't you think? It's serious, really serious! We must help him!'

We didn't really know Old Koukouba that well. Or rather, we thought we knew him, and imagined he must have been born an old caretaker, and would die an old caretaker. As though his end was imminent and certain, we began to learn about his past thanks to the indiscretion of some of the wardens, who took turns in the hut where he lay in bed. These same wardens, especially the nephews of Dieudonné Ngoulmoumako, already spoke about him in the imperfect tense, and extolled some of his good points, but mostly spoke ill of him, for the way he acted in his previous profession.

Should he actually die, Bissoulou Ngoulmoumako said wittily, Old Koukouba would have to be sent to the morgue at the Adolphe-Sicé hospital in Pointe-Noire, where he had worked for over twenty years. Was he exaggerating when he said that Old Koukouba's job there had been to rant at the deceased, according to the circumstances of their death, and then lay them out in boxes, stacked one on top of the other, and sometimes beat them like a rug if they'd died through their own fault? The corpses refused to pass on into the next world, and sometimes dared to wiggle a toe, as though trying to cling to life. When pupils from the secondary schools and lycées visited the morgue with their biology teachers, the moment finally came for Old Koukouba to act like the most important man on earth. With a wicked smile on his lips, he'd make a special show of his corpses, and explain to those present that he had made them look so handsome, it would be a privilege for any cemetery in Pointe-Noire to receive them. Looking at once overwhelmed by his work and passionate about it, he would whisper to his visitors:

'It's been one corpse after another these last few days! This morning two came in, in such a state, I was picking up bits of flesh all the way from the hospital courtyard to my morgue. Apparently there was a bad car crash at the Albert-Moukila roundabout, they were driving flat out, well they're flat out for eternity now!'

His black humour missed its mark with the pupils, who were terrified of the place and of the rigid corpses, so instead he'd say:

'OK, let's not waste time, we'll do a quick tour of the morgue, put on these masks, it doesn't always smell too good in there...'

Old Koukouba then assumed the role of teacher, tenderly cajoling a corpse's shaved and dented head, murmuring in fatherly tones:

'You be good now, my friend, we've got visitors, nothing to be afraid of, they just want to see how we do things here, then they'll leave us in peace...'

As though conscious that the deceased could hear his words, he lowered his voice confidentially and told the visitors:

'The bumps on his head are from a confrontation with his partner's parents. I took pity on him when he arrived here, and managed to hide the worst of it. He keeps complaining about the cold and asking me to turn the heat up, or he won't let his family take him to the cemetery. I'm doing my best to comfort him, telling him he'll get a good welcome up where he's going. But he won't be told, he just sulks, turns over, starts hitting his comrades. The worst thing is, he thinks he's here in this morgue by mistake, some other guy was meant to die in his place, he's got important business to sort out, he hasn't finished paying off his bank loan and he owes money to several people in the Three Hundreds! Yeah, right! The dead have been trying on tricks like this since the year dot, trying to win time, if it was up to them, no one in this world would ever die! It's all very well and good to say it's not your turn to die, what am I meant to do with myself if no one ever dies? And he keeps telling me to fetch his partner from Paris for him. I investigate, and discover the woman in question did go to France on a course for six months, but she got married there to some man who works in our embassy, a childhood friend of the poor corpse here. Hence the fight, which cost him his life, because he got the idea that the parents of his girlfriend were in on the secret of her marriage in France. He got hit over the head with a hammer and died an hour later. Do you think his ex-girlfriend's going to come all the way from Paris for the funeral? If I tell him she's not going to come, he'll get even more difficult with the other corpses! You see what a pickle this job gets me into? It's not just about the burial, the hardest part's the moral support for the deceased. They arrive here in a terrible state, I keep them nice and chilled, I get them up again, I hold their hand all the way to the cemetery, and I'm even the one who digs their final resting place. I told this cheeky corpse, for example, he'd find another wife in heaven, more beautiful than the last, and he asks me if I think any woman up there will have an arse as lovely as his girlfriend's! That's why he keeps gesticulating, wiggling his toe at me, especially when we have company, like now. I'm telling you, it's not an easy job!'

Old Koukouba would forget his visitors were there for a lesson and that stories about corpses told them nothing about the intricacies of the human body, and would not be much help in their exams...

I was surprised at Bissoulu Ngoulmoumako's talent as he imitated Old Koukouba's voice to perfection, not put off by the presence of several residents of the orphanage. It was as though he really wanted to get under the skin of the character, and when he adopted a sepulchral tone, his colleagues all stooped forward to look like old men, so that for us it was just as if Old Koukouba himself was recounting the anecdote from his distant past.

The old warden could have spent his whole life running the morgue, but it all went wrong through his behaviour with the remains of the prettiest girls from Pointe-Noire. In a sense he dug his own grave, because people lost count of the number of young ladies who lost their virginity after they'd died. This was the case with Mandola 'Mannequin', who was still at school, preparing for her baccalaureate in biology at the Victor-Augagneur *lycée*, and would pass it, everyone said, with her eyes closed! She had a Solex moped, of the kind that was popular at the time with the children of wealthy families, and she wore short skirts, tight-fitting blouses, and braids that fell down to her shoulders. One morning, her friends from school, noticing they hadn't heard her moped arrive, learned that the girl mentioned in the news, who had been violently hit by a lorry from the Maritime Company, near the Patrice-Lumumba roundabout, was in fact Mandola, and she had not survived the accident. Before the body even arrived at Old Koukouba's, he heard the news on Radio Dead Street and had laid out a beautiful white dress, shoes and beauty products purchased at la Printania supermarket.

As he washed young Mandola, he talked to her, saying: 'You'll be lovelier than ever! You'll be a white woman, a real one, just for me. The other dead girls will be so jealous, I'll have to find a chamber just for you, I couldn't bear it if they scratched this angel face…'

Old Koukouba got the idea she was his wife now, and for the short time her body was his responsibility he did a certain number of disreputable things, which decency and respect for the dead prevent me from mentioning…

Eight days later, Mandola's family arrived to fetch the body and were just about to take away a different one altogether, which Old Koukouba presented them with as though it was their daughter, in order to be able to continue with his macabre idyll. Out of curiosity, however, one of Mandola's uncles leaned over the next corpse along, that of the 'white lady'. While Old Koukouba had his back turned, busy preparing the false stiff, the uncle took a handkerchief from his pocket and discreetly wiped the face of the 'white lady'. He noticed the black skin underneath, and the two slashes between her eyebrows, the distinctive mark of a sub-group of the Batékés to which the family belonged. His shout of amazement and the echo that followed prompted the entire family group to flee the morgue as if at the appearance of a ghost.

Old Koukouba disappeared through a secret door, escaping the family, who might otherwise have shut him up live in one of the cold rooms. A post-mortem was requested that same day, by the uncle. The next day the front pages of the Pointe-Noire newspapers carried the strangest headlines: 'Corpse rapist who transformed his victims into white women', 'The man who loved cold and inanimate women', 'A love disguised', etc.

To avoid public persecution, Old Koukouba left Pointe-Noire. Disguised as a tramp, he walked for half a day until he arrived in Loango, where he knocked on the door of the orphanage, and presented himself to the religious community which ran it as someone who had lost everything in life, and was seeking sanctuary. He was weeping like a baby, and out of the goodness of their hearts, the religious people opened their doors to him.

He started off working as a gardener and stock-keeper. Then, when the religious community left, and the public authorities took over the establishment, he was appointed caretaker of the premises...

N THE PLAYGROUND, the last of the children playing football were already clearing away as the sun sank below the horizon. I whistled at Bonaventure to join me.

'Moses, why are we hiding in a corner, as if we were plotting to run away from the orphanage?'

I couldn't contain my astonishment.

'So you knew about it?'

'Knew about what?'

'About our escape tonight. You just said it!'

'Really? Some people are going to run away tonight? That's serious. Really serious!'

I could see by the way his eyes stood out on stalks that he wasn't kidding me.

The twins had told me several hours earlier to do a runner with them to Pointe-Noire. I told them I couldn't possibly leave the orphanage, it was my home, even if Papa Moupelo and Niangui had gone.

'So you're going to spend your whole life here, then?' Songi-Songi said in amazement. 'If you're so special, how come no one ever adopted you? And how many children have actually made anything of themselves since you've been in here, you tell me that? None, that's how many. Zero. You were here when we came, you've never gone anywhere, we're giving you the chance to go to Pointe-Noire, and you start acting like you love your masters' house! In fact you probably think we're laying a trap for you, don't you?'

'What if your plan goes wrong and the Director...'

'If it goes wrong it will be your fault!' interrupted Tala-Tala. 'Because you're the only person we've invited to come with us! And I swear that if tomorrow we're still here because of you, you'll die twice over; I'll kill you first, then my brother will kill you all over again!'

They both had their eyes trained on me, as though expecting an immediate response. To gain a bit of time, I stammered:

'What about Bonaventure... I mean, can Bonaventure come with us?'

'What, that imbecile who still goes round acting like a kid? No way!' thundered Songi-Songi. 'He's the kind who wrecks everything, we don't want him in on it!'

His rejection of my best friend gave me a possible way out:

'Well, if Bonaventure isn't coming, I'm not coming either! He's like my twin brother... it's like you two, one can't leave without the other!'

This argument silenced them. They looked at each other, as though conferring on how to respond, then Tala-Tala seized the bull by the horns:

'OK, he can come after all... but if he gives our game away we'll kill him first, then you! Meet us at midnight behind the meeting house of the National Movement for Pioneers of the Revolution. If you're not there on time we'll leave without you.'

'And how are we going to get out of here?'

'Either trust us, or don't bother turning up at midnight!'

They turned their backs on me and went off towards the main building, holding hands, as though they were afraid they might get separated before midnight...

*

'If the twins are running away, that's great, we can relax at last, we'll be the masters of the orphanage!'

'Bonaventure, you don't get it: this is our chance to escape too! Believe me, we won't get into trouble, we'll just say it was all the twins' idea, they led us astray!'

'Who's this "us" you're always talking about?'

'You and me! Don't you get smart with me, time is short!'

He moved his head from side to side a few times: 'No, no, don't count on me, I smell a rat, I'm not moving from here! They want to do like in that film they saw, Alcatraz. They have to be three to get out!'

Unconsciously I repeated Tala-Tala's words:

'Bonaventure, are we planning to spend our whole lives here? If we were such extraordinary children, how come we never got adopted by a family? And how many children have actually achieved anything in all the time we've been here? None, that's how many! We were here when the twins arrived, you and I, we've never been anywhere, and when they offer us a chance to go to Pointe-Noire, you start acting like someone who loves his masters' house! You think it's a trap, is that it?'

'Well I certainly never planned to leave Loango that way!'

'Really? So how exactly were you planning to leave?'

'You know! I'm waiting for a plane to land here, just for me...'

'In Pointe-Noire there's a real landing strip, you'll have all the planes you want when you get there, I promise, you'll be able to fly anywhere you want!'

'That's just smooth talk, don't get me muddled, I'm not coming with you! You go with them, I promise I won't say anything, till the day my plane comes...'

'Honestly! Sometimes I think the others are right when they say you're an imbecile!'

'Oh, I'm the imbecile am I?'

'Yes!'

'Thanks, but I'm not going to just lie down and let you thump me this time, it's over, OK? Finished. Good luck to you...'

He threw me a look like a miserable puppy, then turned his back and walked back to the main building.

For a moment I stood there, wondering if I wasn't about to walk straight into an ambush laid for me by the twins to get me into trouble with Dieudonné Ngoulmoumako. It would be easy for him to get rid of me by explaining to the people in the Congolese Workers' Party that I was just a little local lackey of imperialism. It might even take the pressure off his own hellish situation, and get him back in favour after being edged out by the newcomers. I might get out of Loango only to end up in Boloko, the prison that was said to take only recalcitrant adolescents intent on deflecting their comrades from the path of the Revolution as laid out by our Guide, the president of the Republic.

I only had a few hours left to decide. Should I risk it with the twins, or stay with the person for whom I felt a deep affection? I couldn't see myself leaving without him. And what if a plane did land outside the orphanage one day?

At a quarter to midnight, though heavy with remorse and conscious of the strength of my affection for Bonaventure, I rose from my bed. I looked at him one last time: he was snoring and his left arm dangled from his bed.

I slipped into the corridor and made my way to the meeting place with the twins...

WE WALKED IN SINGLE FILE, and up ahead went Little Vimba, who, in the darkness, seemed about three times our height. I didn't trust him, and I couldn't understand why he had decided to offer us our freedom on a silver platter. Was it because everything in the orphanage was collapsing, and like rats escaping from their holes in a bush fire, everyone was scarpering to save his own skin?

I was forbidden to open my mouth, the twins had been adamant about this: no noise at all, shoes off, moving on the soles of your feet so as not to wake Dieudonné Ngoulmoumako, Bissoulou Ngoulmoumako and Dongo-Dongo Ngoulmoumako. If they saw the structure holding up their empire collapsing piece by piece, they might well do something irrevocable.

There was the exit, straight in front of us, and without turning round, Little Vimba stepped aside to let us pass.

The moment we finally set foot outside, my blood froze: the wardens Mpassi, Moutété and Mvoumbi were outside, each with a club in his hand. They stayed quite still, though, looking off into the distance.

'They're on our side,' Tala-Tala whispered. 'They don't like the Director's nephews...'

I turned around to take a last look at the institution where I'd spent thirteen years. The little light we'd left in the dormitory seemed dull and dim, but in the frame of the window which had just opened, I could see the outline of Bonaventure; he watched us head off into the night, as the heavy double doors of the institution swung shut behind us…

Pointe-Noire

THE TWINS SET A MILITARY PACE for me to follow. I found it hard to keep up. No one spoke, and I broke the silence.

'I still don't understand why Vimba let us escape…'

Tala-Tala explained:

'I guess you think that kind of thing only happens in the movies. Well you're wrong! As you know, for a long time now we've heard Old Koukouba groaning in the toilets every time he pissed. The day before yesterday we plucked up courage and went to tell Little Vimba that we could cure the old man. At first he told us to beat it, but yesterday he came back and asked us how we could cure Old Koukouba when the doctors hadn't been able to. That's when we explained to him that if he allowed us to lay our little hands on the old man, the illness would vanish, just like that. The problem was, Old Koukouba wouldn't hear of it, and we needed to convince him. As soon as he gave us the green light, because Vimba told him he had no choice, he only had days to live, he finally agreed, though not without muttering: "If those two little sorcerers take me for a ride I will take my revenge in hell, I promise them flames that are hotter than the flames of hell!" Little Vimba came to fetch us at dead of night, warning us that if it didn't work he would deal with us at dawn in a way we'd remember for the rest of our lives. We went into the wardens' hut, where the old man looked so stiff we thought he had passed over to the other side. Little Vimba pulled down the sick man's trousers for us, but he woke up straight away and told us we must close our eyes while we were treating him. We placed our four hands by his thing for a few minutes… You know, you won't believe this, but all of a sudden his thing stood up as though he was twenty again. "Step back," he ordered. He had an urgent desire to piss, and urinated in the bucket beside him, regardless of our presence. At first he gave a cry of pain, probably because he was used to doing so by now, then he turned towards us while his steaming urine gushed into the pan. "I'm pissing! I'm pissing normally!" He would have shouted for joy, folded us in his arms, but he had to calm down because if anyone had found us in this situation, with two minors touching an adult's genitals, who would have believed we were only there to cure him? After that, as we'd agreed, Vimba said he would arrange for us to escape, aided by Mpassi, Moutété and Mvoumbi, who were still intent on war with the three other nephews of the Director and even with the Director himself, since he'd appointed the others heads of the orphanage section of the USYC, which may have precipitated the end of Dieudonné Ngoulmoumako's reign…'

I didn't doubt for a moment what Tala-Tala told me. For a long time I had been aware that in our country, twins are born with supernatural powers. At least, I said to myself, they had finally done something useful with their lives, and perhaps the guilt for gouging out their comrade's eye would lie less heavily upon them…

*

We slept in the Grand Marché in Pointe-Noire with some other teenagers we'd found there, each occupying a stall and acting as though it was their own private property. We had to clear out before five in the morning, though, when the market sellers from all over town arrived in lorries with exhaust pipes that rattled like damp farts. The people we feared most were the fish sellers and the vegetable sellers, who, in November, arrived at the weekends around two in the morning. They stared at us from a distance in silence, and their presence alone made us shudder. Legend had it that they actually sold something other than fish and vegetables, that their business was just a cover to mask their sorcery. From November onwards they transformed the Grand Marché into a huge meeting place for the scum of Pointe-Noire and bartered the souls of those due to be 'eaten' during the end-of-year celebrations. This didn't mean tearing them apart and boiling them up in a cooking pot! Each soul for sale was symbolically represented by a fish or a vegetable, and the person who'd been sold would then suddenly fall sick and die without anyone understanding what was wrong with them, despite the attentions of doctors and healers, who all drew a blank. Only the fetishers who came to the funerals were able to 'see' with their third eye that the person had been 'eaten', that his soul had been traded at the Grand Marché and there was nothing to be done…

The fish and vegetable sellers gave us a terrible time if we slept too deep and forgot to get up, because we were exhausted and had spent the day wandering around, pinching meat kebabs from the old mamas who sold them along the main highways, or stealing electrical gadgets from the Moroccan shops on the Avenue of Independence, offloading them quickly in bars, and fighting with rival gangs who objected to our presence in the capital.

The twins' success in seizing control of the Grand Marché

from the other gangs was due to the fact that the people we met there were old friends from the orphanage in Pointe-Noire, who remembered the time the two brothers had gouged out the eye of an older boy. In my opinion, though, that wasn't the real reason they had become big shots in the market. I think it was mostly because they had confronted a young man who had ruled the roost in these parts before we arrived, and was known as Robin the Terrible.

Robin the Terrible was head of the oldest, most organised and feared gang in Pointe-Noire. Before long there was a face-off, and it occurred as soon as Robin the Terrible heard the twins were trying to oust him, and proclaim themselves bosses of his territory. Along with ten members of his gang, he dashed over to Chez Gaspard, the restaurant where we usually spent the day waiting for the customers to give us a few coins as they came out. At that time our gang had only a dozen or so members, most of them little clowns who would never do anything brave unless the twins were at their side.

As soon as I saw Robin the Terrible I felt my legs give way under me, but I tried not to show the twins I was intimidated by him, though he was a big guy, with very dark skin and the muscular physique of a Benin fisherman. I had heard his 'legend' from some boys who'd joined us after being kicked out of his group on one of his whims, which according to them were wildly unpredictable. He was nicknamed Robin the Terrible because he saw himself as Robin Hood, the hero of the Middle Ages, who hid out with his band of brigands in a forest in Europe and robbed the rich to hand out money to the poor. Except that Robin the Terrible had never set foot in a forest and took money from rich and poor alike. The same boys said his obsession with Robin

Hood went back to childhood, when he'd shut himself up in
the library at St Jean Bosco Church after school and read the
adventures of his favourite character, finally putting a face to
his name. He loved the colour illustrations, but he'd get in a
muddle, turn back to the previous page, read it again out loud,
scratching his head, wondering: 'Why is Little John, Robin
Hood's friend, called "little" John, when he's not little at all,
the whole point is he's tall and strong, and he's the chief of the
outlaws in the forest?' A few pages later, he would almost jump
for joy when he realised that Little John had been head of the
outlaws before Robin Hood turned up, and was not going to
yield a shred of influence without putting up a fight. Little John
and Robin Hood were suspicious of each other from the start,
because the cock of the yard won't let a newcomer take over
and give all the other birds the impression he's the one ruling
the roost now. He admired Little John's courage in challenging
Robin Hood to a duel with a stick before the two men became
best friends forever. It was a lesson in survival he would learn
early on himself, and which would later serve him well in the
streets of Pointe-Noire where, if you wanted to gain respect, you
couldn't just shout at someone, you also had to flex your muscles
and defend your territory by whatever means you could. If your
opponent was stronger, then, like Little John, you were better
off smoking the pipe of peace with him, becoming his ally, not
his opponent.

Later, when he quit school, he ran away from his parents'
home in order to live, as he put it, like Robin Hood. There was
a little forest in the Comapon quarter, with just a few mango
and eucalyptus trees that no longer even produced any fruit.
Robin the Terrible would sit at the foot of one of the eucalyptus trees, bored stiff, with not one single kid prepared to

join in his adventure. So he ditched the idea of the forest and took to roaming the streets of Pointe-Noire, since for him streets were like forests too. He made himself a bow, dressed in clothes he claimed were medieval, when in fact he stole them from the flea market on the port at Pointe-Noire, except for the green hood, which he'd had made by the Malian tailors in the Grand Marché and which was much envied. He was the only young bandit in town who went round with bow and arrows. Of course you had to know how to use such a weapon, because although it looked pretty basic it required a lot of skill in the handling, and regular practice, which he lacked. So the very sight of his outfit and his weapon had the bandits of Pointe-Noire, especially the ones at the Grand Marché, fleeing or falling to their knees before him. He controlled the whole territory, and sometimes you would even read accounts of his adventures in the town newspapers.

Songi-Songi and Tala-Tala were a threat to his regime. Robin the Terrible wasn't fooled: he knew that twin-ness conveyed secret powers. For this reason, he came to the twins and asked them to become deputies of his gang.

'Power can't be given,' Tala-Tala replied curtly. 'You'll have to be our deputy, or else fight and show your men you're stronger than us!'

'That's easy to say – you're two against one!'

The twins looked at each other, and Songi-Songi suggested:

'Keep your bow and arrows, we'll fight with our bare hands!'

Those of us in the twins' gang were astounded. Why was he proposing such an unequal contest?

Robin the Terrible leaped at the opportunity and stood poised with his arrow. Before his right hand could even draw back the string of his bow, Songi-Songi pounced on him like a cat and seized his weapon, while Tala-Tala snatched his quiver. It all happened so quickly, we scarcely had time to blink, Tala-Tala was using the arrow to gouge out Robin the Terrible's right eye, while the other members of his gang all turned on their heels in terror and ran. The five or six who were left – too frightened to run – swore allegiance to the twins and joined our gang.

At the sound of police sirens approaching we quickly made ourselves scarce, and Robin the Terrible ran off too, because he knew the police wouldn't care about his eye, they'd just ask him about the various crimes and misdemeanours he'd committed in the town since he'd become a self-styled Robin Hood.

Some time later, Robin the Terrible begged the twins to be allowed to join our gang.

'I'll stop being Robin Hood, but please let me be Little John...'

Tala-Tala answered witheringly:

'You can't be Robin Hood, or Robin the Terrible either. It's over! And you can't be Little John, because we've got a Little John, but we're calling him "Little Pepper", because he proved his worth with pepper, and you'll just be an ordinary member of the gang, like all the rest...'

Robin the Terrible looked like a pirate now, with his little green hat and a piece of cloth covering his eye. But finding himself the laughing stock of those who'd previously trembled at the sight of him, he vanished from circulation. We never saw him at the Grand Marché, and one day someone from his old gang came and told us the body of his former boss had been fished out of the River Tchinouka, having been stabbed and thrown into the water by gangsters from the Mbota quarter, whose chief claimed he'd once stolen his old ma's savings from the Grand Marché...

AFTER A YEAR AND A HALF of living under the twins' protection and carrying out all sorts of jobs for them – stealing scooters or car tyres, mugging whites in the town centre, setting ambushes for lovers near the Martyrs' Bridge, then stealing their purses – I felt increasingly like their second-in-command. I was proud of my nickname of Little Pepper, since it meant they acknowledged I had guts. Lots of people in our gang thought I was called that because I was always sticking my nose into things – or my 'snout', as they said, to wind me up – and was as excitable as a swamp mosquito. It's true, I was in on everything. I was the back-up for all the twins' tricks, and sometimes I was even the unpaid instigator, because afterwards, when they came to divide the spoils, I'd be left like a dog who'd hunted like a mad thing, and got not even a bone from his masters in return.

Since I was their scout, I knew where all the usual suspects hung out, the talentless crooks, the petty thieves who'd get into a scrap at a street party, or steal Michelin tyres, the trainee burglars, the blade-carrying pickpockets, the swindlers with a criminal record so long that the judge would release them after an hour saying, irritably:

'Don't let me catch you at it again! I'm sick of you petty criminals holding up my retirement!'

Not only had I changed physically, I also spoke like the other members of the gang, and had managed to cast off the cultivated speech required of us in Loango. Now I was the one dreaming of being Robin Hood, adopting his name, possessing what had eluded the late Robin the Terrible: that character's generous heart. And if by chance I found a mango thief being chased by some redneck from the Grand Marché, I'd chase the pursuer, I'd helpfully put out my foot and the redneck would go down, while the delinquent, to my huge satisfaction, was able to scarper, jabbing his right thumb at me to express his thanks. This was my way of redistributing riches to the poor, telling myself that these poor gangsters were acting in good faith and were repossessing the goods that had been accumulated by the wicked capitalists in our midst. But the twins put me right on that one, making it clear that unless we wanted all the bandits to throw in the towel, the stuff about Robin Hood had to stop. They insisted on me keeping my nickname of 'Little Pepper', and continuing as their second-in-command, and if they caught me still stealing things at the Grand Marché and handing them over to the poor at the mosque or on the Lumumba roundabout, I'd have to face their anger and get into a fight with them, and risk losing my own right eye…

We accepted anyone in our gang. I got on very well with the paralytics, who thought it was ridiculous, shocking, quite possibly even unacceptable to have two legs; with the blind, who could find a needle in a haystack, or those with only one eye, who took turns to lend each other their good eye, in exchange for meals or a stash of beer.

I'd say to them: 'If you're blind, why don't you make some arrangement with the paralytics, that way they could be your eyes, and you could be their legs?'

But the short-sighted weren't interested in being friends with paralytics and the blind, who were likewise in quite opposite camps. When they ate together, the blind always complained and accused the paralytics of taking all the biggest pieces.

'How do you know we've taken the biggest pieces if you're blind?' the paralytics would say.

And the blind would reply: 'A piece of meat's big if you spend more than forty seconds chewing it before you swallow!'

Then I'd go and mix with other people, like St Francis of a Titty, a twenty-year-old pervert who drew old ladies' breasts on the front of public buildings and claimed it would get him into paradise without waiting in line with all the rest of us, who were too ignorant to appreciate his mammary art. Of all the people at the Grand Marché, he was the most moderate, and I could count on him if I had any problems, even with the twins.

What more can I tell you? There was the stammerer, who kept on repeating: 'Gr-gr-grosso modo doesn't mean perhaps, it means approximately!', and the band made up from the flocks of the Pentecostal churches, furious at their pastors, who'd promised them mountains and miracles and had delivered neither. They maintained that the route to paradise was via the Côte Sauvage, and they went to gaze at it at four in the morning, trying, without success, to walk on the water, because their guru had drummed it into them that since Jesus had pulled off this feat, his worshippers should be able to do it standing on their heads, and let the devil burn in hell. The fire brigade had sometimes had to rescue the faithful when they were drowning and screaming for help, though normally if you're intent on killing yourself you don't go bothering folk who just want to get on with their lives...

WE WITHDREW TO THE Côte Sauvage after a widely publicised operation, led by the town council against the 'mosquitoes of the Grand Marché'. Put bluntly, we were harmful insects, getting in the way of François Makélé, the foremost citizen of the town. He was seeking election for a fourth term, and his picture was on posters at every intersection, all over town. When I stopped to look at one, I was struck by his hypocritical smile, which reminded me of that of Dieudonné Ngoulmoumako two years earlier, when he appeared on the stage at the main building of the orphanage in Loango to announce the Revolution. What mattered to François Makélé was his re-election, and in order to achieve it he used methods of a most spectacular kind. By calling us 'the mosquitoes of the Grand Marché', he had found a way of arousing the antipathy of the entire population against us. On one of the posters for his electoral campaign he was spraying Flytox under the tables at the Grand Marché…

François Makélé took it upon himself to send out militia armed with water guns, coshes and tear gas to deal with us. It was a battle we couldn't win. We were forced to beat a retreat. And thus to help François Makélé remain in his cosy seat, flexing his muscles, and letting it be known that he had succeeded in ridding the Grand Marché of Pointe-Noire of its low-life.

*

On the Côte Sauvage we could breathe freely at last.

We had to prepare our own food, where previously we'd 'helped ourselves' at the Grand Marché. When I say food, I'm talking about cat meat and dog meat, because Songi-Songi and Tala-Tala were of the Bembé tribe and some of their friends were Tékés – that was what the Bembés and Tékés did. If you'd told me I was going to eat meat like that, I'd have given it four seconds' thought before stuffing great chunks of it into my mouth, which had never known wheat from chaff anyway, and had a distinct preference for the chaff over the wheat. As a rule, when you're hungry, your belly will push you to do pretty much anything, and if it all goes wrong inside, unjustly blame the eyes for lack of vigilance. And anyway, I couldn't imagine that the twins and their Téké friends had time to go around doing all this trapping.

I only found out much later that I'd been eating dog and cat food for weeks on end. One day I caught the Bembés talking about a big black cat who always did its business in the sand on the Côte Sauvage and covered it up discreetly. I saw them making a trap which I find it hard to describe here. It was, if I recall correctly, an aluminium pot of some sort, which they'd adapted, closely following a method passed down by their ancestors, with a lid that snapped shut in the second the animal tried to get the bait they'd left inside. They would lure the hapless felines with peanut butter, which cats adore – this is the reason they've chosen to stay domestic, rather than go and live in the bush, where they could live with their feet up, away from the Bembés. Now, cats don't know that true freedom is to be found in the wild. They have clearly never read the story of the town mouse and the country mouse because if they had read it, as I did, in the library at Loango, they would have opted for a life in the bush, where the country mice eat their fill with pleasure untainted by the fear which assails their cousins in the town.

The twins' Bembé and Téké friends made the cats pay dearly for insisting on living with men, and that day at sunset the great black tom made his way to the sea, not to quench his thirst, but to relieve himself and hide his excrement and pee, which since ancient times his species have been ashamed to leave in the light of day, while dogs were happy to spread their shit at every cross-roads, so much so that the mayor, François Makélé, was obliged to put up signs asking their owners to pick it up, or face a fine.

The black tom's big mistake was to always defecate in the same small patch. On that day, then, instead of concentrating on the business before him, his ears and tail stood up on end as he sniffed the pervasive smell of peanut butter on the air. Unable to believe his eyes, or his nostrils, he turned, licking his jowls, and looked over to where we stood, a few dozen feet away from him. He examined the aluminium pot, probably astonished to find it on his little patch. He thought it must have been placed there by the inhabitants so people would stop fouling the place and instead put their rubbish in the bin provided. He also thought that whatever was in a bin naturally belonged to the first animal who came along, and wasn't going to let himself be beaten to it by the horde of emaciated dogs that invaded the Côte Sauvage because in the poor districts of town they were reduced by shortages to eating plastic bags, cockroaches, or on good days, rotting poultry which they had to share with various reptiles, who were dangerous in direct proportion to their levels of hunger.

With a determined leap, the black tom cat found itself inside the aluminium pot, and a short sharp noise could be heard as the lid closed instantly over him.

I still didn't understand what was happening. It's just a game, I thought, to reassure myself. Now the twins were applauding, shouting, kissing the Tékés, and the Tékés were shouting too, and kissing the twins in return, and when they all tried to kiss me, I quickly stepped back, because the reality of the situation had dawned on me. I broke away from the group and began running like a rocket towards the pot to rescue the animal, which was hurling itself about like ten cats in a pot, not one. The twins lurched after my breeches, one of them cut me down, the other immobilised me and landed a punch in my guts. I shut my eyes in pain, and just as I was about to open them, what felt like a hammer blow landed on my nose. It was the one-legged stammerer who was hitting me with the bit of flesh he had left in place of his amputated leg.

As blood spurted from my nostrils, the one-legged stammerer was yelling at me:

'Grosso... grosso... grosso... Grosso modo doesn't mean maybe, it means approximately!'

The twins dragged me along the ground to the place where the cat was held captive and struggling like a devil.

'See this bucket?' Songi-Songi asked me.

'D'you know what's in it?' Tala-Tala added. 'It's our food for tonight! For the last three days we've returned empty-handed from the backstreets of Pointe-Noire. The competition has been getting so much tougher since the elections, you have to do what you can to get by!'

The one-legged stammerer pushed his face into mine:

'And... and... and you can be the one to boil it and carve it up!'

Behind the twins and the Tékés, I noticed the silhouettes of the three strange men we called 'The Three Mosquiteers', because they draped themselves in mosquito nets from dawn to dusk, convinced that the mosquitoes of the Côte Sauvage were only targeting them.

The Three Mosquiteers? There were four of them actually, if you counted their accomplice, the one-legged stammerer, though he didn't cover himself with a mosquito net like the others. Since his other leg was missing, the stammerer couldn't use one of his arms to arrange the mosquito net as it was busy compensating for the absence of his left leg. If he had had the full complement of limbs, he'd have done as the other three Mosquiteers did. That was the evening I realised that we in fact had four Mosquiteers with us, and the fourth, the one-legged stammerer, the youngest and most hot-headed of them, was only fourteen years old...

After the episode with the black cat, I practically stopped sleeping. I kept seeing the look on the creature's face, hearing it meow in despair. I made enquiries of St Francis of a Titty, who was busy drawing a giant breast in the sand, but he gave me a cold reception:

'Watch out for my breast! If you walk on it I'll take your eye out!'

'Actually, I just wanted to ask you about...'

'I know, I know... the cat they ate, it won't leave you alone, right? Listen, you've been eating dog and cat meat for several weeks now...'

'But I didn't realise!'

'We Tékés say: "Never look a goat in the eyes when you eat it – it's sure to look human!" You tried to save the animal, they forced you to prepare it for eating, you got used to its face, and now it's getting to you...'

'Why doesn't the cat haunt the Three Mosquiteers, why is it after me, when I was the one that tried to get it out of the bucket?'

'Because you were more cruel than the Three Mosquiteers...'

'That's not true!'

'Well then, why did you eat a cat you tried to save? The Three Mosquiteers didn't force you to eat it, I saw you take second helpings!'

Confused, I didn't answer. He turned his back on me, muttering:

'Now, stop bothering me, let me finish my breast before the sun goes down... In any case, that cat was a public health hazard, he was getting bigger and bigger, he was going feral, and if he'd gone the whole way and actually turned into a panther, like they do in the villages, he'd have been eating us before we knew where we were...'

I did not intend to spend the rest of my days as a member of this band of cripples, that seemed to expand every week, every month, so that there were some people I didn't even know, and others with whom I constantly argued, in an attempt to assert my authority, since everyone seemed to think they were the twins' deputy, and they never said anything to confirm my position. It was worse than the famous court of the King Makoko, where the monarch just went on snoring while the Batékés partied. The twins had grown distant, sometimes I didn't see them for a whole week. They had stopped working, entrusting certain important missions to new faces who would stick out their tongues and taunt me...

I began to feel almost nostalgic for my former life, and I

was overwhelmed with sadness whenever I thought about my childhood friend. Yes, I wondered what had become of Bonaventure and why he had refused to come with me. We would have been together now. We would have explored the highways and byways of Pointe-Noire. He'd ask those infuriating questions of his, disingenuous but somehow profound. We would celebrate our coming-of-age in two and half years' time.

I drove these thoughts from my mind because I also felt I had been selfish, only thinking about myself, that I should have managed to talk my best friend round, or, failing that, stayed with him – which would have been more logical.

What had happened to the other characters in Loango? Was Dieudonné Ngoulmoumako still Director, or had repeated inspections by the Ministry for Family and Childhood led to his imprisonment? Was Old Koukouba still happily urinating normally, now that the twins had healed his chronic infection?

No, I was done with looking behind me. I had to think about myself now, and immerse myself in my freedom, as I roamed like a wild dog through a town that seemed to crush everything and everyone. But I had to survive, and would devote my energy to that, for after three years spent learning the secrets of this labyrinthine conurbation, I now explored its roughest districts all alone – Bloc-55, Mouyondzi, Comapon, Mbota, Voungou, Mongo-Kamba.

In the course of these aimless meanderings I found myself back in the Three Hundreds, where I met a woman who would change the course of my life. For better or worse, depending on how you looked at it…

I T WAS A SUNDAY AFTERNOON. I was hanging around in the Three Hundreds, not far from the Cinéma Rex, when I ran into a small lady dressed all in red with a white scarf and carrying several shopping bags, just about to cross the Avenue of Independence. Some men playing chequers on the pavement outside the shop run by a Syrian whistled at her, probably because of the way she deliberately wiggled her rear, now up and down, now left to right. It was her way of thumbing her nose at these rude people making indecent remarks as she went by.

I hurried over and offered my assistance. She seemed surprised, probably because the local teenagers didn't do such things. She was worried I might run off with some of her bags, though, and kept turning round every couple of steps to check. To reassure her I drew level with her and we walked along side by side, so anyone passing would have thought I was her boy.

We entered some vast grounds with a big main house and a separate little apartment. Ten girls, each more beautiful than the last, gathered round her and took the bags, which they started to unpack.

'Don't grill the fish too long, girls. And don't overcook the plantains like you did last time. That was disgusting!'

Then, pointing to me, she said to the girls:

'This little chap here helped me carry the shopping without even being asked. Pretty unusual, wouldn't you say?'

They all looked me up and down. I was wearing flip-flops

attached with wire, a faded pair of shorts and a long-sleeved shirt with holes at the elbows. While I was wondering if I should go on standing there like an idiot or leave, though I felt in good company, the woman I'd helped asked me:

'Anyway, what's your name?'

'Little Pepper...'

She looked surprised:

'What kind of a name is that? You must have a real name, like everyone else?'

When I didn't react she sighed: 'Never mind, we'll call you that! My name is Maman Fiat 500!'

She took out a ten thousand CAF franc note and held it out to me.

'Here, Little Pepper, that's for you, buy yourself a shirt and a pair of shorts, what you're wearing looks like you live in a cave, for God's sake!'

The girls burst out laughing, but Maman Fiat 500 frowned:

'Hey, no laughing, OK? It's the first time since I've lived in this town that any boy in the Three Hundreds has been so kind to me.'

Timidly, I mumbled, 'I'm not actually from the Three Hundreds, I was just passing through and...'

'Oh well that explains it!' she interrupted. 'If you were from round here, I'd have been surprised if you'd carried shopping for the *brothel girls*, as they call us – people would give you very strange looks...'

Then stroking my head, she added:

'Come back when you want, treat it like home, isn't that right, girls?'

'Come back when you want, treat it like home,' the girls all echoed in chorus, which made me think of Papa Moupelo's catechism classes, but I banished those images and walked away, without turning round, knowing their eyes were still upon me.

It was the first time in my life I'd been alone with so many women...

That evening, around the crackling fire and the dodgy meat that I wasn't going to eat this time, I told the twins the story of my escapade in the Three Hundreds.

'So, you're saying a *tart* gave you ten thousand CFA, right?' said Songi-Songi in amazement.

'Usually other people give them money!' said Tala-Tala, amusingly. 'Show us the note then!'

I took it out of the pocket of my shorts and Songi-Songi at once snatched it from me, twisting my fingers.

'You haven't paid your subs for two weeks!'

I felt this was a bit unfair, as they had been absent from the Côte Sauvage for these two weeks. And ever since their return they'd been taking in subscriptions from the gang members. I parted with my ten thousand CFA francs without demur...

A FTER THIS, I WENT every afternoon to visit Maman Fiat 500 and her 'girls', as she affectionately called them. I stayed in her yard for hours at a time, and was happy whenever she sent me off to buy drinks for her clients, or contraceptive pills, French letters or medicine for period pains.

One day, when we were eating together in her apartment, I revealed to her, without being asked, that contrary to what she and the girls still believed, I wasn't just another teenager off the streets of Pointe-Noire but had run away from the Loango orphanage almost three years ago now. I confessed my real name was *Tokumisa Nzambe po Mose yamoyindo abotami namboka ya Bakoko*.

She almost choked on her mouthful of manioc:

'What idiot lumbered you with a pretentious name like that?'

I told her about Papa Moupelo and the dance of the Pygmies of Zaire. I unconsciously did the movements to the dance as I told her how Papa Moupelo used to do it. Maman Fiat 500 nodded her head at this, and began to move her shoulders and, catching me off-guard, sprang up and started shaking her hips, lifting her arms high above her head, emitting a deep-throated cry and then freezing like a statue, with her wide eyes fixed upon me! That she was nimble of foot should not have surprised me, considering she too was from Zaire, like Papa

Moupelo, probably of the same ethnic descent, so it was natural she should dance the dance of the Pygmies, rather better, I must say, than Papa Moupelo. She danced it with grace and subtlety. Perhaps because she closed her eyes, enabling me to admire her body in movement, the perfect 'O' of her rear, as though swiftly drawn with a compass, the chest with its two large, ripe fruits that anyone would have longed to pick and bite into.

I talked to her, too, about the socialist scientific Revolution that had come knocking at the doors of the orphanage and brought about the sudden end of an era. She looked grim as I described Sabine Niangui, her maternal kindness, and the way she cared for me up to the moment she disappeared. The thought of Old Koukouba and his painful urinary infection also touched her. My voice suddenly grew louder, with an edge of contempt, as I recalled Dieudonné Ngoulmoumako and his nephews, the corridor wardens.

Maman Fiat 500 looked at me so directly, I gradually lowered my voice and withdrew into myself, eventually falling silent. A few tears trickled down my cheeks. She wiped them away with the edge of her *pagne* and then she too began to speak.

As she did so it became clear she was a born storyteller, modulating her voice as though to summon up my emotions:

'You know, Little Pepper, all the men who've had me in bed have offered to live with me, to leave their wives and children. They've promised me castles, Mercedes, and goodness knows what else, but I know pleasure makes people say things they regret in years to come. That's one thing that never changes, men will say anything when they're in your arms. Let me tell you now, this body of mine has been touched by the filthiest cart-pullers as well as by the top officials in my own country, and in this country too. This business is my life, it's what I know how to do best, little one, and it's what has brought me here to this country. The day I can't do it anymore, I'll pack my bags and return quietly to my native land, back to my village of Bandundu, where I'll work the soil and watch the cycle of the seasons. I never had children, my seven brothers all left Kinshasa. Three of them live in Brussels in the Matongé district, and married white women; two of them manage to make a living in Angola, in the food trade, and the last two wander about the metro in Paris busking illegally, or so I've gathered from people back here on holiday. It's as if there's a wall between us, in their eyes I'm just the black sheep of the family. I never hear from any of them, perhaps because they resent me for following in our mother's footsteps...

She paused, as though to check I wasn't shocked by these revelations.

'Was it really her fault? Only God can judge our acts, Little Pepper. Does anyone ever stop and wonder how a woman comes to sell her charms? Do they think it's an activity you choose like any other, like becoming a hairdresser, or a carpenter? A woman isn't born a tart, she becomes one. There comes a day, you look in the mirror, there's nowhere to go, your back's to the wall. So you cross the line, you offer your body to a passerby, with an empty smile, because you have to seduce the client, like in any business. You tell yourself, you may debase your body tonight, but tomorrow you'll wash it clean, and restore its purity. So you wash it once with bleach, you wash it twice with alcohol, then you stop washing altogether, you accept your acts as your own, because no water on earth ever gave anyone back their purity. If it could, surely with all the streams and rivers and seas and oceans there are on earth, all men and women here below would be pure and innocent. I simply followed the destiny God saw fit to give me, even if all anyone sees in me is the madam who

controls the girls she's brought over from her own country. My
father abandoned us when I was a child, and my mother brought
me up to this trade, which she plied herself till the end of her
days. Thanks to her we had a roof over our heads, my seven
brothers and I. While the girls in our village were playing with
their dolls, my mother was already explaining to me how to hold
on to a man: cooking and sex, she said, the rest is an illusion,
including beauty. A beautiful woman who can't cook and yawns
in bed will soon find herself supplanted by an ugly woman who
can make a good dish of saka-saka and give her lover a great
time.'

In time I learned that Maman Fiat 500, properly known as Maya
Lokito, got her name because when she was working in Zaire
she had a small vehicle, a genuine, white Fiat 500. She was proud
of her car, one of the rare models made in the 1950s, which
remained fashionable until well into the 1970s, designed by an
Italian, a certain Dante Giocoas, she told me. It was a gift from
one of her most illustrious clients, an opponent of the President
of Zaire's regime. Said opponent, Wabongo-Wabongo III, lived
in Brussels and was so mad for her, he'd visit her four times a
night whenever he was staying in Brazzaville, our capital city,
and had only to cross the River Congo on the sly to see Maman
Fiat 500 in Kinshasa.

Even in our country, Wabongo-Wabongo III had to stay
hidden, because our President and the President of Zaire
conducted little opponent swaps from time to time.

The first time the President of Zaire thought he saw Wabongo-
Wabongo at Maman Fiat 500's, he couldn't believe his eyes. He
asked the four aides crammed into an unmarked car with him:

'Did you see what I saw? That guy leaving by the secret

door down there, on the other side, do you see him? Isn't that Wabongo-Wabongo III, the idiot opponent who tells lies about me in Europe?'

His henchmen answered calmly: 'No, Mr President, Wabongo-Wabongo III lives in Brussels, he hasn't been allowed into this country for seventeen years, we have your presidential decree here in the glove box.'

He glanced at the decree, recognising the signature:

'You're right, that is my signature... But even so, are you quite sure that wasn't him I just saw?'

'Absolutely sure, Mr President! We've heard Wabongo-Wabongo III, that son of a whore, is sick in Brussels and can't even afford to pay his hospital bills, they even say he's trying to appeal to your kindness and get you to pay his mountain of bills! Ha! Ha! Ha!'

'Oh yes, that's right, I did hear about that, how silly of me! Well, that dumb ass will get nothing from me, he can go ahead and die in Europe! I'd rather pay his funeral bills, it'll cost the state less money!'

They laughed heartily, and his aides praised the President's sense of humour, which, they said, could always be relied on. They also noted what they referred to as the 'the President's witty gems'.

But after a moment the President stopped laughing and came back at them again, as though he'd suddenly been stung by a swamp mosquito:

'Hang, hang on guys, no, no, there's something not right here... You're telling me it's not Wabongo-Wabongo III I've just seen? OK, but a man has escaped out the back there, and if it's not Wabongo-Wabongo III, that lousy opponent of mine, then who is he, you tell me that? Isn't that what I pay you for?'

One of the men, the smallest of them, who always had an answer for everything, tried to calm the President:

'Mr President, perhaps I could just point out that there are a lot of girls here…'

'So?'

'It's their business.'

'So?'

'Well, there are lots of girls, and lots of men come to see them, and leave by a secret door for privacy, it happens every day…'

'Yes, but there's only one Maya Lokita in there! Anyway, you're getting on my nerves, you always have an answer for everything! Hell, that's why you're so short!'

'I do apologise, Mr President…'

'I know you've got a degree in Political Science from Paris, but don't think that's going to impress me.'

'I don't think that, Mr President…'

'Let me tell you, I was in Indochina with the honourable President Gnassingbé Eyadema.'

'Of course, Mr President.'

'And I'm sick of little men, from tomorrow you're sacked, you can give back the black Mercedes and your villa! Find me a tall man, preferably without a Political Science degree for God's sake! It's not rocket science, what I'm asking for right this moment: I just want to know who that guy is who just left Maya Lokito's, my Maya Lokito's, is that crystal clear?'

Since the short man with an answer to everything just stood there with tears in his eyes and said nothing, the tallest of the four ventured to say:

'Mr President, I don't have a Political Science degree, and I am taller, I'm one metre ninety-three… With your permission

I'd like simply to remind you that your Maya Lokito is the girls' boss, she's yours and yours alone, Mr President. She only does it with you, no one else gets to touch her. But she must eat, she must provide for herself as set down in the Constitution, which you yourself drew up with such wisdom and insight, and I quote, still with your permission, the sublime article 15 of our Supreme Law: *Citizens, male and female, must make their own living and not expect any help from the Founding Father of the Nation...'*

The President started in surprise:

'That's very badly written! Are you sure that's in my Constitution? *My* one?'

'It's in your Constitution. *Your* one, Sir. Moreover, article 17, modified by...'

'All right, all right, spare me your opinion, Mr of No Fixed Diploma! You studied for every single diploma there is in France, you didn't get a single one, but you've still got the nerve to open your mouth and talk about the modification of my Supreme Law, my law? Did I ask for your opinion?'

'No, Mr President...'

'Well then, don't open your mouth unless what you've got to say is better than silence, for God's sake! I know my law, because it's *my* law, and I *am* the law!'

'Absolutely, Mr President...'

'Let's get back to serious matters: who is that guy I saw coming out of Maya Lokito's place, if it isn't Wabongo-Wabongo III? You do realise, don't you, he spends his whole time criticising me, in collusion with the whites, who are jealous of our diamonds? And now he dares show his face around here!'

Another bodyguard timidly stepped up:

'Mr President, if I might just...'

'How tall are you?'

'One metre sixty-three, but I get up to one metre sixty-seven when I wear platform shoes, the ones you get from the Moroccans and Syrians in the town centre...'

'And what did you say about the man who slipped off when he saw us?'

'Well, Maya Lokito's running a business here, with these girls...'

'And?'

'What I mean is, there are other clients, who come for these other girls...'

'And? I still don't see the connection!'

'These clients have to pass through Maya Lokito's private room.'

'And why's that?'

'To pay for their trick, they don't pay the girls directly...'

'Hang on, hang on, hang on...You're not so stupid after all, you're better than all of them!'

'Thank you, Mr President...'

'In fact, this changes everything!'

'Mr President, we ought really to be more discreet and not wait around here too long, even if our car is unmarked. Either we should leave or you should go in and find your Maya Lokito...'

'You're right... But how come I never noticed you were so smart till now?'

'Because my colleagues are all taller than me, it's hard to see me, especially when I'm walking behind them...'

'But why have you been hiding your intelligence and letting these other imbeciles shoot their stinking mouths off?'

'They're my bosses, Mr President...'

'Well from this moment on, you're their boss!'

'Thank you, Mr President.'

'I have to go now.'

'Go ahead Mr President, we'll cover you as usual.'

A few days later, the President came back again, with the same henchmen, and, seeing the same thing happen again, realised it really was Wabongo-Wabongo III, who had managed to get back into the country over the water, via Angola and Cabinda Province. The four men were first fired for an attempt on the security of the state, then liquidated without trial.

Four new guard dogs now accompanied the President when he visited Maya Lokito, with the secondary mission of laying a trap for Wabongo-Wabongo III, who was caught the day after the delivery of a Fiat 500, which his opponent had given to Maya Lokito, who from then on would be known as 'Maman Fiat 500'.

As Wabongo-Wabongo III was stepping out of Maman Fiat 500's shack, two henchmen grabbed him, immobilised him and forced him to swallow hemlock.

'At least he will have had a philosopher's death,' cracked one of the henchmen.

It was being said across the water – and the news soon reached us too – that Wabongo-Wabongo III had died after a long illness in a hospital in Brussels. The President for life, in his infinite goodness, added the communiqué, would pay the funeral costs and elevate this noble son of our country to the rank of hero of the Red Revolution…

✳

After we'd each made our confession, Maman Fiat 500 served me a dish of manioc leaves with squashed bananas, a speciality of her native Zaire. It was because of this dish, she joked, that there were so many divorces in our country, because only the women from Zaire knew how to make it, and once a married man had tasted it, he would leave his wife for a 'true woman of Zaire', she said, with a broad smile.

That day I slept for the first time in the living room of her apartment, and when I got back to the Côte Sauvage the next day, the twins looked severe. They read me the riot act, but after a moment Tala-Tala calmed down again:

'In fact it would even be good if you spend most of your time there, it would suit us!'

They explained that if I lived at Maman Fiat 500's, I could be their spy, their look-out, and I could supply them with the house keys of all the pot-bellied, bald-headed bourgeois from Batignolles, where they had as much electricity and drinking water as you could want. I could also obtain valuable information by listening behind doors when these rich guys were whooping it up at Maman Fiat 500's. I'd hear them chuckling after a few glasses of Sovinco red, boasting that they'd been to Paris, Rome or Moscow. They owned several houses, they'd add, in all the big towns of our country, and were going to buy a yacht so they could sail at the weekends, their house in Pointe-Noire was the finest in all Batignolles, and their neighbours were European, or close family members of the President of the Republic.

Under pressure from the twins, I crept into Maman Fiat 500's apartment and stole her clients' keys and went to get copies made by the locksmith, Pata Koumi, a couple of blocks away. He'd give me a long hard look, hesitate for a moment, as though sensing I was up to no good. But I had an argument that usually worked: I'd tell him I'd been sent by Maman Fiat 500, and he'd set to it straight away, which gave me some idea of her influence in the neighbourhood, and how much she was trusted. I paid the locksmith with tips I'd been left by these same clients two or three days earlier and the next day I'd go over to the Côte Sauvage and hand the keys to the twins, so they could then get on with organising things.

The two brothers asked Massassi Kalkilé and Lokouta Elekayo to go and do the recces, which might last weeks, during which they'd play cat and mouse with the owners of these sumptuous buildings. The twins insisted they draw the residences, and as Massassi Kalkilé and Lokouta Elekayo were not necessarily great draftsmen, Songi-Songi would get angry:

'Is that meant to be a house? Where are the doors and windows?'

So the twins gave them a Polaroid camera which they'd pilfered from La Printania, the supermarket, and explained how it worked by taking photos of some of us.

'Don't smile, it's just to try it out, it's not a real photo!' they'd tell us.

So we set our faces rigid, convinced this would make us look like proper gangsters...

UNLIKE THE TWINS and the other boys on the Côte Sauvage, I could now boast an adoptive mother and a roof over my head, which should have gradually distanced me from my rootless existence. However, as I was in some way cursed, or determined to hold on to a part of my past, I continued to meet up with my acolytes during the few hours when Maman Fiat 500 was busy cuddling her big fat clients. And since she had some every day, I could meet up with the gang and hand over to Songi-Songi and Tala-Tala a portion of the tips I'd earned at Maman Fiat 500's.

In the gang, each of us was obliged to contribute to the kitty kept by the twins. It could be this was where things first started to go wrong, because I got the feeling I was contributing more to the group than the others and receiving nothing from it. What did the twins do with all the money that came pouring in? They explained that it would be there to help any one of us if we got into difficulty. What kind of difficulty? It seemed suspicious to me that the twins should suddenly develop a concern for humanity. Now I understood why they 'worked' less and less and had taken a bit of a bourgeois turn. Why should they shift themselves when others could do their dirty work for them?

My suspicions were well-founded. The twins disappeared with the kitty and the whole group broke up, each of us free once more to act alone or just to become a normal teenager.

But I was angry with Songi-Songi and Tala-Tala.

I reckoned they'd stolen from me, and ought to give me my money back. I looked all over Pointe-Noire for them, with a knife hidden in the back pocket of my shorts. For over a month I searched the Grand Marché and the Côte Sauvage with a fine-toothed comb and questioned the members of other gangs. No one had seen them around there. But I somehow had the feeling that I'd end up running into them, I'd manage to corner them some day, and demand that they pay me back at once. I cursed myself for not having recognised their deceit, and for having wronged Maman Fiat 500 by stealing her clients' keys and handing them to people who didn't deserve it. But such was their charisma that, face to face with them, you dropped your gaze and did whatever they told you. Would I be able to resist?

WAS SIXTEEN YEARS OLD and now living at Maman Fiat 500's. Had the good Lord been willing, I too might have known Cleopatra, beloved of Julius Caesar and Mark Antony, and met the sulphurous Messalina, who I'm told prostituted herself in broad daylight, in the streets of Rome, and transformed a corner of the royal palace into a house of worse-than-ill-repute, venue of orgies equal in every way to those held in our own Maman Fiat 500's kingdom. But it wasn't the will of the Good Lord that I should enjoy the favours of these illustrious ladies. The girls who worked for Maman Fiat 500 talked to me, however, and confided in me more than they did in their clients.

I can still see them now, each with the nickname given her by Maman Fiat 500: Féfé 'Rear entry guaranteed' Massika, Lucie 'Volcano fire' Lembé, Kimpa 'Magic caress' Lokwa, Georgette '5a.m. Nutella' Loubondo, Jeanne 'Crumbly biscuit' Lobolo, Léonora 'Instant decapsulation' Dikamona, Colette 'Venus of Milo' Wawa, Kathy 'Midnight Tornado' Mobebisi, Pierrette 'Eleventh Commandment' Songa, and Mado 'Spaghetti waist' Poati. It was with the last of these that I had my first sexual experience, which I won't go into here, because it was a disaster: I was so anxious and stressed that the moment she touched me down there I felt as though everything was falling from under me, my body dissolving and as though something might suddenly come out of the end of my sex. The worst thing was that afterwards she made fun of me, telling Jeanne 'Crumbly Biscuit' Lobolo and

Léonora 'Instant decapsulation' that I had no control, and that the moment she touched me I was already 'finished'…

It's true, of course, their skin was worn, they wore blonde wigs or red – sometimes green or mauve – but their clients were happy, even so, and, as Maman Fiat 500 said herself, the men felt like they were kissing the queens of the Crazy Horse or the Moulin Rouge in Paris, no pig in shit could have been happier. And so they poured out the filthy details of their ruined marriages to these queenly ladies, snivelling at their feet because their lives no longer formed a perfect four-sided figure with four perfectly equal angles. I listened to them with ears wide open, because they were happy to talk to me, Little Pepper. And I saw it all as from a distance, fascinated by the kisses given by these women, who got married at least twenty times a day to men who were good fathers, whose scooters were tidily parked in a little side street, or more often, in a mean little passage that led down to the River Tchinouka. They were discreet in that way, and often their wives would come and burst the tyres of their Yamahas, or Suzukis, or pour sugar into the petrol tanks of their vehicles. I laughed like a drain in my corner, in Maman Fiat 500's straw hut.

I can still see them now, all lined up in a row, these girls with their multi-coloured *pagnes*, their make-up copied from a fashion magazine, their false nails, their bright, messy lipstick that left an indelible kiss on the back of the regulars' jackets and shirt collars, their fake blue or green eyes that turned reddish at sunset, their cheap ladies' heels that made them move like a rhino on the run from a poacher, their handbags where they kept condoms and thongs next to Mananas and Joli Soir perfume, along with a traditional *pagne*.

I can still see their dirty tricks, four or five men who all turned up at once, each one pushing to go first because he's got a mohair or alpaca suit from France or Italy, and it was a massacre. Maman Fiat 500 was beside herself, running round in circles, fire-fighting, trying to get the belligerent ones to take a different girl, but everyone wanted Féfé 'Rear entry guaranteed' Massika.

I can still see them now, when they'd given themselves to a man that they trusted, who'd promised to come back the next day at dawn – the famous payment in kind, or quid pro blow, as Maman Fiat 500 called it. And the bastard never came, went a different way round, avoiding the neighbourhood, until the day his domestic supply got cut off after a stupid row about the food in his plate, and then he'd be back with his tail between his legs, his eyes on the floor, and his wife in the wrong and still as plain as the nose on her face. And when the girls saw him coming, they came out of the yard, with their claws sharply drawn, a regiment of harpies, pushing him away, flinging obscenities, before throwing water in his face, full of little chilli peppers, prepared by me, and reminding him that gorillas of his sort belonged in the bush, not here in the Three Hundreds.

*

Every day I witnessed the same scenes: suspicious clients – usually married men – came in through a secret door, the important ones ushered into Maman Fiat 500's apartment. I studied their attitude, especially those who, noticing my presence in the building for the first time, pretended they'd lost their way, that they'd actually been looking for the bistro *Black Angels Have Small Dicks*, which was right opposite and nobody could miss. And Maman Fiat 500 came out of her apartment – she always kept an eye on what was happening on the Avenue of Independence – took the strays by the hand and whispered:

'No, there's no mistake, you've come to the right place, you don't want the bistro if you're looking for a good time!'

Then she signalled to the girls who led them into the centre of the courtyard, installed them under a straw shack and served them some St Pauli beers.

Some of the clients still hesitated, muttering:

'I should actually explain, I was just wandering aimlessly through the neighbourhood, I saw a light, and I said to myself: "Well, well, well, there's a light over there, even though the whole neighbourhood's cut off." And then, if you see what I'm saying, I came over without even thinking what I was doing. Oh well, I guess I'd better be getting back…'

Then Maman Fiat 500 would reassure them:

'Make yourself at home, no harm in having a bit of fun…'

Then she'd call to me:

'Little Pepper, fetch me some St Paulis from across the way for these gentlemen…'

I liked to sit at the entrance to the building with Likofi Yangombé, a porter who had failed at his career as a boxer in Zaire. He lashed out with a stick at any undesirables who tried to peep through the breaks in the wooden fence at what was going on inside the enclosure. As soon as he saw me, he felt the need to tell me the tale of his glory days, in particular the little details of what happened before a fight:

'You just can't imagine how stressed you get before a fight! All you can think of is the sequence of punches you've been taught in training. Left, right, left again, right again. Then there are the legs. I know what I'm talking about, son. You don't win a boxing match with your hands, you win it with your legs! They have to be light, help you fly, support you, and follow the rhythm of your arms. You try it one more time in the changing room, then you have to go, and you slip on a robe with your initials on the front, and your whole name printed on the back. You start dancing about, to warm up. In a few minutes, with your hands carefully wrapped up, then placed in Everlast gloves, you make your way down an interminable corridor, with your team following behind. And at last it's there, waiting for you, far away at first, the ring, a little elevated square with ropes around. And there's a roar, and the hall is plunged into darkness. That's where the showdown takes place, before an excited crowd of people roaring for or against you...'

*

In the morning the girls each took up their position outside the room they'd been assigned by Maman Fiat 500 and waited for me to bring them their breakfast. I didn't mind doing it, because I knew I'd be allowed to eat with them, and if I'd followed the promptings of my own greedy stomach I'd have eaten ten times a day, because the girls gave me ever more affection and my way of saying thank you was to go with them to market, or to the clinic in Mouyondzi where Maman Fiat 500 sent them every month for intensive medical check-ups.

In the evening they were more aggressive, and stood outside the front gates, protected this time by the three cousins of Likofi Yangombé, while he pretended just to be having a drink opposite, at the *Black Angels Have Small Dicks*, intervening whenever some joker came and bothered the girls...

ON THE DAY BEFORE my nineteenth birthday Maman Fiat 500 found me a job as a dockhand down at the port, thanks to one of her most regular clients, Rigobert Moutou. Head of personnel at the Maritime Company of Pointe-Noire (MCPN), he came three times a week, parking his scooter inside my 'mother's' lot, and passing me a thousand CFA franc note for looking after his vehicle. Then he'd go and join Maman Fiat 500 in an apartment separate from the main house where the girls lived and worked.

One day, as he left Maman Fiat 500's apartment, Rigobert Moutou whispered to me:

'Come to the port tomorrow, I'll put you on a salary, that way I won't have to give you a thousand CFA francs every time I come.'

I knew this was Maman Fiat's idea. She worried about my future and was sick of me hanging around in her courtyard year in year out, wandering from her apartment over to the main house, where sometimes I would intervene between three or four girls who were about to get into a fight. I expect she'd had enough of me being the kid who helped with everything, waiting to be sent to buy beers in one of the nearby bistros when clients arrived. From now on I would work, and gradually detach myself from her, that must have been what she wanted, because a month after I'd been signed on she gave me the keys to a little place she'd just acquired down by the River Tchinouka.

It was just a little patch of land with a hut made of boards. Her plan was to build a large house, and the hut was there to ward off the crooks who went round selling off vacant land in the town as though it belonged to them.

So my job was to watch over the property, but it gave me some autonomy, even if I regularly went back to Three Hundreds to look in on Maman Fiat 500, say hello to the girls and check no one was trying to make trouble of any kind for my little adoptive family...

*

I was an exemplary worker. At least, that's what my colleagues said. Why else would they have kept me on for ten years, until my state of health went and ruined it all? I would probably have become chief dock hand, and possibly one of the most important people running the whole port, who knows?

I got up early to go and wait for the MCPN lorry at a bus shelter in the Avenue of Independence, opposite Vicky's Photo Studio. The vehicle stopped at every intersection, other dock hands piled on and we travelled along in silence. The lorry discharged us like sardines by the roadside at the entrance to the port and we walked up to a barrier where men in uniform checked our identity, confiscated our bags and finally let us pass. That was the start of our long, harsh day – unloading the containers under the watchful supervision of the foremen, as they suspected us of stealing objects brought in from abroad, and getting rid of them in the evening, on the streets.

My colleagues were astonished at my petty stealing:

'Do you want them to send you back to school or what? If you're going to get caught with stolen goods, you might as well get caught with something worth having!'

Any poor wretch caught red-handed was taken to the main customs office, a tiny little room that smelled of cat's piss, with rats the size of papayas crossing from one corner to another, knowing they'd never be trapped because they were just part of the scene, and also because many people in the town considered killing an animal equivalent to attacking an ancestor, incurring the wrath of the spirits who are supposed to protect the living and make sure that they're welcomed into the next world on good terms. The rats understood this, which explained the indolence of their movements, and why they didn't even stop to check they were safe with strangers.

This was the office where they stripped the workers naked before lashing them with barbed wire and imposing a settlement of accounts which made them debtors for the rest of their lives. We feared coming up before the floggers, who would beat the culprits impassively, till blood flowed, and the louder they cried, the harder and longer they hit them. It was a sort of summary tribunal with no chance of redress: they'd heard that you'd stolen, there would be no investigation, but you'd be punished and fired. I saw family men down on their knees, pleading for forgiveness, weeping and pissing into their shoes while the flogger stood there unmoved.

At one o'clock in the afternoon, we finally got a break in which to eat. The foremen, with the floggers in tow, watched us like hawks throughout. They lived in fear of confabulations and transactions, and were therefore opposed to the idea of workers eating together. At each table they posted a guard built like a weight-lifter, chewing on great chunks of manioc, flicking his eyes over us, alert to the faintest whisper.

In the evenings we were only allowed to leave the port after interminable searches in which we were stripped down to our birthday suits with our hands in the air, in the customs office we referred to as 'The Filter House'. On re-emerging, we felt like we'd passed an exam.

I was considered above all suspicion: together with an old customs officer, I stole ring-bound notebooks and pens. He was known as Papa Madesso Y Bana. To avoid being checked, he would bring the notebooks and the pens to my hut in the evening. I'd give him a ten thousand CFA franc note to help feed his nine kids, three wives, three official mistresses and a litter of nephews whose names he could never remember because he always mixed them up with his own brood.

MPENETRABLE ARE THE WAYS of the Lord, Papa Moupelo would have said. What with my little job at the port and my regular visits to Maman Fiat 500's, I seemed to be leading a normal life, when with a great fanfare, the mayor, François Makélé, the same one who had already driven us back to the Côte Sauvage with his famous 'Grand Marché Mosquitoes' operation, now launched 'Zero Zairian Whores in Pointe-Noire'. You'd have thought life was one long election campaign. He wasn't actually running for mayor this time, but for the Presidency of the Regional Council of Kouilou. The tricks were the same though: choose a group to gang up on, and wage a noisy campaign, preferably with aggressive involvement of forces of law and order and the TV cameras. The 'Mosquitoes' had completely disappeared from the Grand Marché, which had now grown so big it extended as far as the Rex district. In these circumstances, a campaign against the new 'mosquitoes' would mean driving all the kids of Pointe-Noire out of their own town. So operation 'Zero Zairian Whores in Pointe-Noire' fitted the bill, because it left the Congolese whores in peace and meant the mayor could boast about killing two birds with one stone: eradicating Zairian prostitution in the town, at the same time as fighting illicit immigration, since many of these women had come to Pointe-Noire via Angola or Cabinda Province, using couriers who had sold them Congolese identity cards…

In the town, then, everyone was talking about the witch hunt against the call girls from Zaire, and many people were concerned about the inhuman way it was being conducted, even if a large part of the population welcomed the initiative. How could they justify bringing in bulldozers, borrowed from construction companies, to destroy the majority of brothels in Pointe-Noire, while soldiers went round coshing the poor women, and transporting them in 4 x 4s to the Police Head-quarters at the Lumumba roundabout to check their visa status? The interrogation they were subjected to was a mere formality, for in the end, whatever their situation, they were beaten up, and sometimes raped by a band of policemen...

Imagine my surprise the day I turned up at Maman Fiat 500's to discover a field of rubble, as though a bomb had suddenly wiped everything out during a war with the Americans! I thought I must be hallucinating, a feeling exacerbated by a sort of darkness that descended on my soul. The shock was so terrible, I stood staring at this scene of destruction for over an hour, wondering what had become of Maman Fiat 500 and her ten girls.

When at last I came to my senses, I went to the town centre, where the Angolan and Cameroonian girls mostly worked.

I couldn't find Maman Fiat 500 and her girls anywhere. I took the return bus back to my cabin, which from now on felt like the only link between me and my little family, who were without a doubt on their way home to Zaire. I paced up and down my tiny patch of land. I was at my wits' end, I'd lost all sense of time, and it was probably around then I started to feel gaping holes in my head, hearing noises, like all these people running around inside it, echoes of voices from empty houses, voices not unlike those of Bonaventure, Papa Moupelo and Sabine Niangui, the twins, but most of all of Maman Fiat 500 and her ten girls. After that, nothing. I remembered nothing, not even who I was.

HADN'T BEEN BACK to work for weeks, and several of my colleagues came knocking at my door, to try and bring me back to my senses. In a fit of panic I threw hot pepper water in their faces. I didn't recognise them, I thought they must be garden gnomes trampling all over my poor little spinach plants, when all that was left for me now was to cultivate my garden in a corner of Madam Fiat 500's plot of land. I could handle anything, except people coming and messing up my precious little spinach plants, which I watered with joy.

I'd leap from my bed very early, as though I was going to go to my place of work. I'd make sure a lorry from the Maritime Company hadn't dropped off any gnomes in the garden, I'd fetch a pick and a hoe, a spade, a rake and a watering can, which I filled with water from the River Tchinouka. Then I'd whistle as I dug the soil and scattered seeds. Sometimes I'd just sit the whole day long in my vegetable plot, hoping to catch my spinach plants growing. I was actually worried they might pop up when I wasn't looking and I'd feel like a fool next to my neighbour, Kolo Loupangou, an old man who liked to think he was an expert gardener, just because he'd got his technique and his gardening know-how from learned works devoted to the art.

Kolo Loupangou, who refused to plant anything but lettuces, asked me:

'Is your spinach coming up?'

I replied:

'Yes, my spinach is coming up.'

'If your spinach is coming up, does that mean my lettuce will?'

'No, your lettuces won't come up!'

I said that to get rid of him, so he wouldn't stand there looking at my spinach plants, distracting me, dragging me round to his way of thinking, talking to me about his old books. One of these books was called *The Theory and Practice of Gardening*, published by one Dezallier d'Argenvile in the 18th century, Kolo Loupangou explained. And he added that this Dezallier d'Argenville was a great garden lover, even if he was actually a lawyer by profession.

To be fair, I should admit that it was thanks to him that I'd switched my garden from one side of the plot to the other.

Kolo Loupangou had come over to see how I was getting on, and exclaimed:

'You're wasting your time Little Pepper, your garden is in the wrong place, it won't flourish, there's something important missing!'

'Really? What's that then?'

'In *Country House*, Countess Genlis, or perhaps I should call her Stéphanie Félicité Ducrest de Saint-Albin, points out that the kitchen garden should always be close to the dwelling and close to the dung heap. So you need a dung heap!'

And he helped me with this initiative. I was shocked to observe that he was burying cow dung and all sorts of disgusting things in my soil.

'You see, the worse it smells, the better it is for your dung heap,' he assured me.

The book he was most proud of had been published by Olivier Serres in the 17th century, with a title as long as your arm: *Theatre of Agriculture and Field Management… in which all aspects of the art of cultivating and exploiting the land are set out with clarity and precision, in consideration of its various qualities and climates, both as expressed by the Ancients and acquired through experience…*

'This book is my bible.'

He immersed himself in the reading of this book for a whole half day, roaring with laughter as he did so. According to him, gardening was an art I would never understand because I didn't have green fingers, because all I could grow were pathetic little spinach plants right by my house wall.

Although he said I lacked gardening experience, he admitted I managed quite well, conceding:

'Yesterday, as the day declined, I was sitting in my doorway and I spied you with your old man's rags, seeding with open hands the furrowed earth that will yield harvest in the months to come. Perhaps you don't know it, but you were trying to imitate that famous and august gesture of the sower, whose tall dark silhouette o'ercasts the fields, his heart set on the fruit of passing time.'

I understood nothing of this outburst, which was doubtless taken from his reading of ancient books. But I knew he was a kind man, and that it must be a compliment, since he said it all in a warm, kindly voice.

A few weeks later, when I was still savouring his compliment, and my memory troubles were getting worse, he saw me in my garden and ran across:

'I haven't seen you imitating the august gesture of the sower since this morning! What are you doing, standing there among your spinach plants?'

'I'm watching them grow.'

'What do you mean, watching them grow?'

'There's something I'd like to understand, and your books say nothing about it: why do my spinach plants only grow when I'm not watching? I find it unacceptable!'

'You're right. It is unacceptable.'

'It's ungrateful of them! Who is it that waters these poor little spinach plants? Who looks after them? Who pulls out the weeds that stop them growing? I won't let them do it to me! I'm not leaving this garden until my spinach plants make up their minds to grow here and now, before my eyes!'

Kolo Loupangou gave me a long, sympathetic look and murmured:

'Little Pepper, I'll be frank with you: I think you need help. Your situation isn't just serious, it's completely and utterly desperate…'

For years he would continue to sing this refrain, as my memory problems affected my gait and I started to walk in zigzags because it completely slipped my mind that the shortest route from one point to another is a straight line, which is why, as they say around here, drunkards always come home late.

The minute I set foot outside my cabin, I'd get lost. I wandered all over the Côte Sauvage, because I actually thought my little house was on the other side of the ocean and I just had to walk across the water, a bit like the famous messiah whose exploits of this kind are all recorded in the Holy Book. Each time I tried to perform the same trick – I was very curious to know how this guy pulled it off, even urging one of his disciples to do likewise – I held back, muttering to myself that the water was too cold, or too polluted with the excrement of certain locals who claimed it was fine to relieve yourself in the sea because the wise men of our country had shown that salt kills all known germs, even the most resistant, the ones that hide deep down in the ocean.

Hither and thither I went, not realising that I kept looping back through the same spot. In my head I heard the waves booming, and when they broke I had the feeling everything around me was exploding, and I would be swallowed up by the sea. So I stuffed my fingers in my ears and stopped myself breathing for several seconds, till the waves disappeared and I could say to myself that it wasn't the sea that was coming to get me, that I was the one who was haunted by its presence.

*

The illness affected more than my walk: judging by my attire and my actions, people thought I must be a ghost who'd been thrown out of the Mongo-Kamba cemetery, or someone who might cross swords with his own shadow, and end up in profound disagreement with it over which way to turn at a crossroads. Dogs crossed my path and immediately fled, barking at me, to be on the safe side, from several hundred metres away, outside their master's plot. So I saw that the best way to get rid of a dog was bark yourself. I've met dogs who were so astonished by – and possibly admiring of – my mimicry, they broke off barking and lay down before me, as though accepting me as leader of their pack...

For protection in the dry season, I went round covered in a thick woollen blanket and a straw hat, carrying a long wooden stick to frighten the children, whose game was to pelt me with stones. I tried running after them, but they were so quick and agile that in no time they vanished from my sight. My new physical appearance made it difficult, even for my neighbour, to recognise who I was.

Because I was going round and round in circles, like a snail caught in the spiral of its own slime, I needed some little trick for working out where I was when I went wandering. Using my stick, I drew a cross of Lorraine wherever I went, to avoid doubling back the same way a few minutes later. As a result, several alleyways were marked with multiple crosses of Lorraine, since I had as much right as anyone else to walk up and down the public streets, even though I didn't pay taxes – besides, if only people who paid their taxes were allowed to use them, then God help us, our neighbourhood streets would be as empty as those in a deserted town in the Wild West.

'Well I never, a cross of Lorraine! So I've been this way before, I'd better go a different way, where there are no crosses of Lorraine!'

I'd change direction, but some young wags decided to put crosses of Lorraine everywhere. I got more and more lost, because I couldn't tell my crosses of Lorraine from those of the jokers, who were as inventive as they were annoying. So I gave up drawing crosses of Lorraine, and spent my time rubbing them out instead.

Some afternoons I'd do a tour of the town's cemeteries, enjoying a spot of butterfly-chasing with a sling. I visited the tombs of Loandjili, Diosso, Fouks, Mpaka, Mbota and Mongo-Kamba, with the idea that my biological mother, who I never knew, was buried in one of these tombs. Not that I felt the need to discover who my true mother was, or why she left me at the orphanage of Loango a few days after my birth. What I really wanted was to spit on her grave, and ask for an explanation. Since I didn't know if she was actually dead or alive, I railed against all the dead people in the cemeteries, resting in peace and enjoying people's respect, while I was out here suffering. I scratched out the inscriptions on the crosses and wrote in other names instead. I admit now that because of me the families of the dead often got lost in the rows of a necropolis, and knelt down at the graveside of people they'd never known. And to cap it all, I would stand there cackling between two gravestones, not realising that only decency and courtesy stopped the unknown departed from telling me to go to hell.

As if this wasn't enough, at the time of the full moon, especially in leap years, I was determined to get to see the navel of a policeman's wife. The idea haunted my sleeping and waking thoughts. It got so bad, I started drawing on the ground what I thought the navel of a policeman's wife might look like, instead of crosses of Lorraine. I was pretty sure I'd seen all sorts of navels in our neighbourhood, and even in our town, but I'd never seen the navel of a policeman's wife.

When I passed a woman, any woman, in the street, I'd ask her if her spouse was a policeman. She'd always stare at me in astonishment:

'Are you off your head, or what? Asshole!'

At long last, a woman took pity on me. She'd seen me hanging around in the street for hours, asking women for their husband's profession, never finding one who was married to a policeman. One day she stopped and told me that her husband, Fernando Quiroga, was a well-known lawyer/estate agent with an office in the centre of town.

'Your husband's a lawyer, not a policeman!' I said, rejecting her approach to me outright.

'Policeman, lawyer, it's all the same thing...'

'No, it's not the same thing at all, one carries handcuffs, the other doesn't, he snaffles the worldly goods people leave their heirs when they die!'

'Can I just show you my nice little lawyer's wife navel anyway?'

'I want a policeman's wife's navel, and that's that!'

I read both disappointment and humiliation in her face.

After a while I gave up on this, because I heard about a guy who died of a heart attack in the arms of a policeman's wife when at long last she showed him her navel...

returned to the Côte Sauvage after many long years to find all the old vagrants had gone, and I felt like the oldest of them all.

'That guy going "I've lost my memory", he's an interloper, he'll denounce us to the police!' some of them said among themselves.

I swore I wasn't in cahoots with the police. That I'd gladly return to my shack, but how would I get there?

'You don't know where you come from then?'

'Yes, that's right...'

'But you *do* remember that you don't know where you come from?'

The young ones on the Côte Sauvage all thought I didn't know what I was saying, that I was really just a mental retard. I put up with their cruel remarks, but I wouldn't let them say I was a loser, that my incoherent words and behaviour recalled the primal utterances of our prehistoric ancestor back in the day when by mutual consent he divorced our cousin the monkey, because he was sick of him and had discovered he could go it alone, and light his own little fire using two flints rubbed together instead of wolfing down raw meat like a savage. A number of these false friends already had me dead and buried in a nice white shroud, so when they saw me reappear with my Don Quixote de la Mancha look, they decided I must be tilting at windmills or running after a simple peasant woman, my heart's own desire.

So they all shouted:

'Look at this imbecile, he doesn't even know where his shack is!'

So they all turned away from me. One of them said to me in a voice full of scorn:

'You know what your problem is, Little Pepper? Your visceral stupidity has paralysed your mouth. Its grip on your circumvolutions tightens daily. You talk to yourself, you think electricity pylons are magical giants you must fight by hook or by crook. One look at you and it's quite clear, man truly is descended from the monkeys!'

This was really too much, so I answered back:

'One look at you and all doubt goes, luckily for you, and unlike me, you are not descended from a monkey, but you're catching up so fast, the human race will have a whole new species of primate before you can say "light year"!'

The creep then yelled:

'You want my fist in your face or what? You old asshole! The cemetery's the place for you, why are you still alive, when real people are dying all around you? What are you even doing in this town? What are you even *for*?'

And he walked away, showing me the middle finger of his right hand, pointing up towards the sky...

I RECALL IT WAS A BLISTERING afternoon. We were packed so tight in the Pointe-Noire Public Transport bus, that when people jabbed me in the ribs with their elbows, I jabbed them back just as brutally, until my neighbour, Kolo Loupangou, told me to calm down, behave properly, and above all not to show people that I had a long-term problem, a really big problem, here in my head. He also spent the whole journey marvelling at how he had cornered me like a rat near the Côte Sauvage, and dragged me along with him, when he hadn't seen me in my shack for several months and had been searching in vain in the remotest districts of Pointe-Noire.

While I was busy complaining about the heat and smell of perspiring passengers, Kolo Loupangou waxed lyrical about the doctor he was taking me to:

'You'll see, he's just great, I promise! He's the only doctor who can treat diseases of the brain in this town, and quite possibly in this country! I don't know what the hell he's doing in Pointe-Noire, if I were him I'd have stayed in France, in Paris, and got paid as well as the white doctors! Doctor Kilahou saved Kaké Ebeti, an old bugger in his fifties, who'd been wandering naked through the streets for over twenty years and apparently had a centipede in his brain. He wouldn't give a hurricane lamp to his maternal uncle, and his uncle was so bitter, he asked evil spirits to destroy the majority of his neurones! Doctor Kilahou did neutralise the mystical centipede, but first he got Kaké Ebeti to kneel before his uncle and buy him the hurricane lamp he'd been wanting for years. These days the old madman lives like a lord: he's married to an ex-Miss Rex, wears suits from Europe with ties that outshine the rainbow and to top it all he's landed the post of personnel manager at Printania supermarket! The same could happen to you Little Pepper!'

I didn't know what to say to this, I was more interested in the two bottles of beer I'd hidden in the sand by the Tchinouka, to keep them cool till I got back. The more I thought about it, the more I imagined these two bottles getting pregnant, having lots of little baby-beers, who one day would also have baby-beers, till my whole world was just one great ocean of alcohol.

When the bus stopped opposite the building of the National Water and Electric Company, my neighbour heaved a sigh of relief:

'This is where Kilahou's surgery is, inside this fine building belonging to the NWEC.'

In the lobby, Kolo Loupangou halted by the lift:

'He sees his patients in private, and I respect his way of working. That's how he cured Kaké Ebeti!'

'Are you leaving then?' I asked anxiously.

He pointed over at a little room in the corner of the lobby:

'I'll wait for you there, to make sure you don't disappear again for months. I won't move till you come down!'

'I don't want to talk to someone I don't know, he'll just upset me for nothing and…'

'Please, just be polite, don't talk to him like you talk to your friends from the Tchinouka and the Côte Sauvage, he's a doctor, he's studied with the whites!'

He stepped inside the lift with me, pressed the button, and stepped out again before the doors closed.

I saw him settle onto the sofa and lunge at a jar of sweets on a coffee table.

As soon as the lift doors opened on the first floor, I leaped out, convinced I was finally escaping a trap. On one of the doors on the landing, on the left, was a gilded plaque that declared:

DOCTOR LUCIEN KILAHOU

Neuropsychologist
Faculty of Medicine, Paris
Intern, Hospitals of Paris
Enter without knocking

I knocked anyway before entering.

An old lady with legs like a wader bird, wearing large spectacles, looked me carefully up and down before letting me in.

'The doctor will be with you in a moment, he's just talking on the telephone.'

'I'm in a hurry, Madame!'

She shot me a look like a pistol:

'You don't have an appointment, and you're in a hurry? Well then, why don't you make an appointment for another day if you're in such a hurry today?'

While I was having a good look at her blonde wig, which only just covered about two-thirds of her skull, I was muttering to myself, inside: 'Calm down, Little Pepper, your neighbour's waiting downstairs, don't disappoint him.'

Embarassed by my staring at her, the woman attempted to move her wig forward a little, to hide a few grey hairs that were showing. She handed me a year-old newspaper and asked me to take a seat in an enormous waiting room with walls covered in pictures comparing from every possible angle the brain of a human with that of an elephant, a dolphin, a gorilla, a cat, a dog, a chimpanzee and a mouse.

I looked at the one of the human. It was terrifying to think that we're walking around with compacted mush in our heads. For the first time, I learned the terms for the different parts of the organ: mesancephalic duct, thalamus, hypothalamus, the pons, fornix and pineal gland. I imagined the assistant, who was keeping an eye on me from the reception desk, taking off her wig every evening and extracting her brain, to give her cranium a good clean before putting everything carefully back in place.

I brushed these thoughts aside and opened the newspaper I'd been handed on arrival. As the photo of the mayor, François Makélé, occupied half of every page, I closed it again, and threw it on the floor. At a distance, my eyes met those of the assistant, who appeared not to appreciate this gesture.

After a quarter of an hour, a short, obese man, with a bald head, came over, and held out a damp hand towards me. I refrained from giving him mine, and asked him suspiciously:

'You work here too, do you?'

'I'm Dr Lucien Kilahou…'

I didn't greet him in return, not because his hands were sweaty, but because he wasn't wearing a white blouse like a real doctor but rather sported a *pagne*-like outfit with shiny embroidery around the sleeves and neck, which gave me migraines.

'Please step this way, sir…' he said.

He led me into another room with fierce air conditioning and white walls. He gestured towards a leather seat, and sat down opposite me with his arms crossed over his paunch. My attention was caught by a framed photo on the wall just behind him, the only picture in the room: on one side of the doctor stood a white woman, on the other a plump, mixed-race adolescent girl, who looked exactly like him.

'I've spoken to your neighbour, whose relative I cured, a few times on the phone. Your case interests me... I suggested he should bring you here, without an appointment, if ever he got hold of you. Clearly it hasn't been that easy, it's taken months! Anyway, I know about the difficulties you've been experiencing for some time now, and I can confirm that your neighbour has considerable respect for you...'

'Yes, but he's stayed at home!'

'No, he's waiting for you downstairs in the hall... Look to your left.'

And sure enough, on a little black-and-white screen which I hadn't noticed before, you could see the whole of the ground floor lobby and Kolo Loupangou cramming himself with sweets.

The doctor stood up, went over to switch off the screen, and came to stand in front of me again:

'Right, I'm going to ask you a few questions...'

'Questions?'

'In our jargon we call it SEMQ, or "Self-evaluation memory questionnaire". I try, if possible, and necessary, to adapt my questions to the patient and the realities of our country.'

He placed a pile of pictures before me, opened a notebook, and for over half an hour, questioned me on the names and faces of famous people in the Congo, the country opposite, France, black Americans such as Muhammad Ali, George Foreman or Martin Luther King, my childhood, the orphanage in Loango where, a week after my birth, the parents I never knew had dropped me and run. That was when I realised that my neighbour had given him some very precise details concerning my life.

The doctor then focussed his attention on everyday tasks, directions to get to the Rex district or the Three Hundreds or Savon or Tié-Tié, current affairs, items of vocabulary in French, Mumkutuba, Lingala, etc. As soon as I answered, he put a cross on a form which I couldn't read, because he had his big damp hand over it. I realised he was giving me marks, and that in the end my replies would tell him what was wrong with me.

My irritation with the doctor's questions increased as the exercise went on.

'Are you a man or a woman?'

Without hesitating, I replied:

'It depends on the day, on the month.'

His moustache, which till now had been drooping, suddenly perked up in surprise.

'And today – are you a man or a woman?'

'Both, maybe. I don't know, I've lost track...'

'And what is your name?'

'Little Pepper.'

'I meant your family name, not your nickname...'

'That's what people call me, and if you haven't got a family there's no point having a family name... I'd have preferred to have a nice name! A name that sounds good!'

'Really? Like what for example?'

'Robin Hood...'

'Why Robin Hood? That's not a Congolese name, to my knowledge!'

'It would take too long to explain, doctor...'

'I want to come back to a question you didn't answer: what is the name of the President of our Republic, the Father of our Nation?'

'François Makélé...'

'No, François Makélé is the mayor of Pointe-Noire, and I asked my secretary to give you a newspaper with his photo on every page. She told me you threw the paper on the floor. Why did you react like this?'

'It was an old newspaper. It was from a year ago!'

'I know, but we don't elect a new mayor every year...'

To cut short this interrogation, in which the doctor seemed to feel the need to correct me every time, and answer on my behalf, I changed the subject:

'What about the injections?'

'What injections?'

'You see, doctor, I only have to look at a syringe and I'm finished, I'm out like a kite.'

'What do you mean, out like a kite?'

'Isn't that the expression?'

'Mister Little Pepper, there will be no injections, not today, at any rate, and with me you won't be out like a kite, as you put it.'

'What about next time?'

'Sufficient unto the day...'

'What do you mean by that?'

'That will depend on the results of the tests I give you.'

I began to feel he was making fun of me when he stopped smiling and stared at me as though I was from a different planet. When a doctor looks at you even for a few seconds without speaking, it's like he's been looking at you for an hour and is hiding some alarming diagnosis from you. So you feel obliged to say something. Yes, I expect that was his technique for getting patients to confess.

'I'm aware I've been a little slower than usual. I'll try to speed up a bit...'

He showed me two objects sitting on a little table behind me.

'Do these two objects mean anything to you?'

I turned round and glanced briefly at them:

'No, nothing!'

'Mister Little Pepper, I must ask you to adopt a more co-operative attitude, and to take your time…'

'They're still useless objects!'

'Why do you say that?'

'Who put them on that table anyway? Do you really think they belong here, in an office?'

'Listen, I'll be frank with you: I'm not here to amuse myself! I studied in France, let me remind you, just in case you didn't read it on the plaque outside my door! Just give me the names of these two objects and we'll move on!'

I didn't let his change of tone intimidate me:

'I don't know what they are…'

'Look at them carefully one more time!'

'No, no idea.'

'Everyone has these, you must have them in your own home! You must remember!'

'No, I can't!'

'You *can't* or you *won't*?'

I straightened up and adjusted my shirt collar:

'If you're going to be like that, I'm leaving!'

'Mister Little Pepper, what I want to hear is: "That's a spoon, it's for eating soup and liquid food; and that's a pot, it's for cooking food in!" It's not exactly difficult to say the name of an object and explain what it's for!'

'Shall I tell you what my real problem is, doctor?'

I could tell he was thrown by that, then he went on:

'Go on then, I'm here to listen.'

'My illness goes back a long, long way…'

'Meaning?'

'I'm ill because of my adverbials...'

He burst out laughing:

'That's the first time I've heard that one! Where did you get that one from?'

'A friend said it, his name's Strong-as-Death...'

'All right, but what have your psychic problems to do with adverbials?'

'Well, let me ask you, doctor, what is the role of adverbials in a sentence?' Embarrassed by this question, he looked down, stifling another shout of laughter:

'I must admit, you've got me there, I've never really thought about it...'

'My friend Strong-as-Death told me that the purpose of the adverbial is to complete the action expressed by the verb, according to the circumstances in which it is undertaken. Which means, if I'm not mistaken, that without it, the verb is fucked, it can't express cause, means or comparison etc. with any degree of precision. Perhaps my memory is no longer reliable because I've lost most of my adverbials! Or maybe I don't know where to put them in my sentences! If my adverbials aren't there when I need them, I won't be able to remember the time, place or manner etc., and my verbs will be all alone, they'll be orphans like me, which means I'm getting no information about the circumstances of the actions I perform. Strong-as-Death thinks I could pick up some adverbials in the street, because some people just throw them away when they've used them, but I'd need to pick up some that correspond to the ones I've lost. Which would be difficult, because I'm not the only person looking for them in this town and even when I find one, it never seems to be the same as I had before, so I...'

'All right, that's enough!'

'Because...'

'I said that's enough! I'm a doctor, not a French teacher.'

'I was honestly trying to help you, doctor...'

'Let's try something simpler. What is the most recent memory in your head right now?'

'Now?'

'Yes, right now.'

'You mean, apart from my adverbials, which you've just crossed out, so my verbs are left all alone?'

'Don't you worry about that, if you answer my question your adverbials will be back in no time.'

I thought for a moment, then I said:

'All right, I remember that the day before yesterday, in the late afternoon, I saw some gnomes trampling the poor little spinach plants in my garden. And what do you think I did? I chased them away, because, if you can put yourself in my shoes for a moment, my poor little spinach plants hadn't harmed them, all they'd done was grow, and it's me that waters them morning and evening. That reminds me, I mustn't forget to water them tonight...'

'Gnomes in your garden, you say?'

'Yes, real garden gnomes. They were talking, like you and me! There were even some twin gnomes, and I can assure you, you don't get that very often these days!'

'You wouldn't by any chance be mistaking your friends from the Tchinouka or the Côte Sauvage for garden gnomes?'

'No, they were real gnomes! They had mouths, arms, noses, ears and something dangling down between their legs, if you know what I mean. There were lots of them. One of them, the oldest, I think, was dressed as a customs officer and was talking about having to feed his ten children and nephews.'

'And how did you get rid of them?'

'I threw hot pepper water at them, and they escaped in a Maritime Company lorry.'

'Your neighbour tells me you used to work at the Maritime Company…'

'I wasn't just anyone!'

'And these gnomes, did you see them when you were working at the port too?'

'I'll say! I was their boss, their immediate superior! No gnomes in charge of Little Pepper!'

'What about you, Little Pepper, are you a gnome too?'

'Some days yes, some days no. And if I compare myself to a dinosaur, then yes, I'm a gnome…'

'Let me get this right – you've seen a dinosaur?'

'Honestly, doctor! Who *hasn't* seen a dinosaur? There are loads of them in the Tchinouka! And contrary to what most people think, dinosaurs are sweet and lovely if you don't provoke them…'

'You smell of alcohol… do you drink a lot?'

'About average…'

'Meaning?'

'A case of beer a day. Hang on though, I don't mean on my own! I'll give you names if you want!'

'No, it's OK…'

'Because I wouldn't like you to think that I'm the only person in this town who likes to have a drink now and then. There are lots of us down on the Côte Sauvage, especially by the Tchinouka, you can check if you like, everyone brings his own case of beer. Except maybe Mokila Ngonga,the carpenter, he's older than the rest of us, he doesn't drink beer, only whisky, he says beer gives you a belly and when you have a big belly you can't see your organ to get hold of it for a pee. And also…'

'And have you been drinking today?'

'Yes, but I didn't drink it all, I hid two beers in the sand when I saw my neighbour coming to get me to bring me here, and I'm hoping those two bottles will make lots and lots of baby beers!'

I paused for thought, then added:

'No, I didn't drink it all, but it doesn't matter, even when I haven't had a drink, I feel as if I have: I'm lucky that way, it's as if my body stores the alcohol. My friends often compliment me on it, they say I'm a one-man brasserie!'

I was laughing to myself, when the doctor murmured:

'I think I can see what may be wrong with you…'

'Wait a minute doctor, it isn't just the gnomes that bother me…'

'What is it now? An army of giants?'

'Just the last few moments I've had an image in my head of this big black cat we ate…'

'What? You ate a black cat?'

'I didn't want to hurt him, it was the Bembés who caught him and ate him like it was just normal meat, when it really wasn't!'

'Well one thing's certain, you've a vivid imagination, Mr Little Pepper!'

'I swear it's the truth, doctor!'

'I could sit here listening to you for hours, but we need to get back to reality…'

The neuropsychologist launched into a series of convoluted explanations, which I listened to without reacting. I heard terms which were every bit as complicated as the ones I'd read in the waiting room, each more amphigorical than the last: Alzheimer's, agnosia, anterograde amnesia, retrograde amnesia, antero-retrograde amnesia, lacunar amnesia or selective amnesia...

At the end of this string of gobbledy-gook, he concluded:

'I wouldn't be surprised to find we're looking at Korsakoff syndrome...'

I almost leaped out of my seat:

'Who's this Korsakoff?'

He remained calm and said:

'Sergei Korsakoff was a 19th-century neuropsychiatrist. One might consider it ironic that someone like him, who devoted his life to diseases of the brain, should have died at forty-six of a heart attack! Who knows, perhaps if he had been a cardiologist he would have died of the illness that bears his name today!'

Seeing me looking a little lost, he went on:

'To put it simply, you probably have some complications arising from Wernike's encephalopathy... I will however need to carry out a more detailed diagnosis. Some preliminary signs lead me to believe that this is what we're looking at: you have been drinking excessively for many years, you find it difficult to remember things from the past and to assimilate new ones, if your story of the gnomes that haunt you, or the black cat you ate with your friends are anything to go by, you have a marked tendency to fantasise...'

'So doctor, you're saying I'm just a liar...'

'I'm not accusing you of anything, Mr Little Pepper, I'm looking for a diagnosis and at this stage it's just conjecture. Having said that, I'm rarely wrong about this syndrome, it was the subject of my doctoral thesis in France, which I obtained, incidentally, with distinction. Let us say that after I've run some tests on you, we will have to consider a long course of treatment, a very long course of treatment indeed...'

Accompanied each time by Kolo Loupangou, who, when he wasn't snoring on the couch with his feet up on the coffee table, sat waiting for me in the lobby and stuffing himself with sweets, I went back for several weeks for further consultation and analysis, after which the doctor confirmed that my 'neuropsychological assessment' was 'serious', and I had 'advanced cerebral lesions'.

He was looking shifty, which made me anxious, and I felt my heart sink into my stomach when he concluded:

'I don't want to hold out too much hope, because your condition is irreversible… However, I am going to prescribe some medicines for you to deal with the side effects…'

'I'm not ill, doctor!'

'People like you who suffer from attacks of amnesia usually succumb to what we call anosognosia, a state in which they deny that they have the illness…'

He advised me not to drink any alcohol, not one single drop, and put me on a diet which he wrote down on a piece of paper. I passed out each time he gave me a powerful injection of vitamin B1…

Throughout the treatment, Kolo Loupangou stuck to me like a limpet, but at least he didn't tie me to the foot of a mango tree, the favoured approach of most Pontenegrins to cure the mentally ill, before eventually dumping them in psychiatric asylums. Many a time and oft I've seen madmen bound hand and foot with string, which they gnawed at nervously, while barking as though they were actual canines. Faced with this humiliating spectacle, dogs would stop for a moment before the wretched captives, pricking their ears up, unable to figure it out.

Each time I came back down to the lobby after my consultation, my neighbour said:

'I'm very proud of you, Mr Little Pepper, you slept in your shack yesterday. I'm most encouraged, it means the treatment's starting to work. I will come and fetch you again next week, now don't disappear again, you have your health to think of now!'

My neighbour was perhaps too optimistic. Three or four months later, we still seemed to have made no progress. Doctor Lucien Kilahou was so exasperated by my rudeness, he asked me never to set foot in his consulting room again. Again and again I called him a gnome, or even Pygmy. I talked to him about the adverbials I'd picked up in the street, but which weren't the ones I was looking for. I told him about my desperate struggle with the gnomes of the Maritime Company, who were demolishing my spinach plants. I also mentioned the black cat we'd eaten, whose meows grew ever louder inside my head.

'You are the rudest patient I've ever had in my consulting room. Korsakoff syndrome does not excuse everything!'

'I've made some progress, doctor, even my neighbour says so...'

'No, you always smell of alcohol, even though I ordered you to stop six months ago! I didn't say anything when you turned up drunk, but there are limits, and you have just exceeded them!'

'Give me one last chance, doctor...'

'There will be no last chance, you've blown them all and now I am asking you to leave this consulting room! I know I took the Hippocratic oath back in Europe, but I don't ever want to see you here again, you're an imposter!'

I remained in my chair, feeling my anger rise.

'Get out of here or I'll call the police! And you know where they'll put you? In an asylum!'

The word 'asylum' echoed so loud in my head, I stood up

swiftly. Before I left I yelled at him exactly what I had been thinking for the last few moments:

'You don't give a shit about me, you haven't since the very first day! Well, see if I care, you're not the only doctor in this town!'

Just as I was leaving his consulting room, I noticed that the utensils he'd used for my tests were still sitting on the table at the back, and I took malicious pleasure in saying to him:

'Do you know why one of those utensils is called a *marmite*? Because *marmite* doesn't just mean "cooking pot", it's also the old French word for a hypocrite. It's a hypocritical container, just like you are, you don't know what's inside till you lift off the lid! You're just a *cooking pot*, doctor! And what the hell do I care about spoons? Do you know that in the past people used a shell for a spoon, especially for eating snails? Which of us is the snail, do you think, and which the spoon?'

'Get out of here!'

When I got back to the lobby, my neighbour saw the look on my face and asked in alarm:

'Did you have more injections than usual?'

'I'm never coming back here anyway, he threw me out because of the cooking pot and the spoon, that's how he catches his patients out!'

To my great surprise, Kolo Loupangou was even harsher with the doctor than I had been.

'This guy's only any good when someone has a centipede in their head. It's not a centipede you've got in there, it's something else, only a traditional healer could rake through your memory and put everything back the way it should be…'

KOLO LOUPANGOU no longer escorted me, as the healer he had chosen lived by the Tchinouka. Sometimes I went to see this healer five or six times a day, and he'd say:

'Little Pepper, what are you doing back here again? You were only here at midday!'

'Was I?'

'We ate together at midday, as usual. Don't you remember?'

His name was Ngampika and he only required payment if he cured you completely, which, he added in a rush of self-satisfaction, white medicine could not guarantee. The sign at the entrance to his plot probably had more writing on it than any other sign in town.

Healer Ngampika
Direct and legitimate descendant of King Makoko
Former personal sorcerer to the mayor, the prefect and the
President of the Republic
Specialist in incurable illnesses, both known and unknown
Guaranteed return of errant wives within 24 hours
Complete cure for sterility, impotence and hernia
Meals provided throughout treatment
Payment after total and definitive cure

I felt comfortable with Ngampika. He was an affable little old man who said 'tu' to me right from the start and I could have a laugh with him over a glass of palm wine, because white men's science, according to him, was full of incomprehensible terms and devoid of effective cures. I kept saying I really mustn't overdo the palm wine:

'Doctor Kilahou said that I've got Korsakoff's syndrome, and apparently that also comes from drinking...'

'Little Pepper, that doctor told you a load of porkies! Kwashiorkor is a children's illness! Everyone except him knows that! He studied in France too long, he must have left his brain behind! Do children drink alcohol? And yet they're the ones who get kwashiorkor in this country!'

We got so drunk, and laughed so much, that Ngampika would forget that I was there for a specific reason: to recover my memory.

'Come on, just one more little one! Let's drink to the health of our ancestors, and up yours doctor Kilahou! Come back again tomorrow and we'll start the first consultation then. Give me a night to have a chat with the ancestors and you'll see how we get on!'

The day of the first appointment, I turned up at his place looking neat as a new pin. One of my friends by the Tchinouka had cut my hair with a Gillette razor blade and another had lent me his clothes.

The healer congratulated me:

'How well-dressed you are! Though I don't know what idiot did your hair, they made a mess of it, it's sticking out all over!'

With his chin he indicated the six sinister-looking masks suspended above our heads:

'Have you seen those masks?'

I looked up anxiously:

'They're so ugly! They look like monsters!'

'You be careful, they're listening to us, I've spent the whole night talking with them...'

'Have you now!'

'You won't get better without their help.'

'And how are they going to do that, they'd have to get themselves down from there and...'

It was as if an insect had stung him. His eyes turned red and bulged out of his face and he launched into a long tirade:

'Listen, dialogue with masks isn't your area, it's a job for Ngampika, the exceptional being sitting opposite you now! I am the direct and legitimate descendant of King Makoko, first cousin of King Mâ Loango and distant relative of the royal family of Rudolf Doula Manga Bell, whose son, Doula Manga Bell, when he became King, was hanged by the Germans in 1914 because he opposed the urbanisation project whose aim was to dispossess the Doula people! The Doulas were Congolese, like you and me, my friend, except they were always on the move, and in the 16th century, after they'd had enough of moving around, they made a settlement near the estuary of the Wouri, which would later become the town we know as Doula! That's why, when I go to Cameroon to buy a few *gris-gris* for my hernia – I mean the kind of hernia that makes your testicles swell up bigger than a papaya – I'm able to speak Doula without an accent! Let me tell you this, Little Pepper, my ancestors were rich, they had gold, many wives and shedloads of slaves. And what did they do with it all? They gave their entire fortune away, sharing the fate of those who suffer, helping them, interpreting the messages of our spirit ancestors! These masks represent my riches, and I'm not in this business to make money, if I were I wouldn't be the only person who asks for payment on complete recovery only, while the doctors in this country get paid by the social security even when they don't achieve a cure! Does that seem right to you? If you give your car to a mechanic round here, do you pay him even if he doesn't fix it? It's unheard of! They can teach you anything in these schools of medicine, here or anywhere else, but the spirits of our ancestors will forever remain a mystery. Starting today, tell yourself that your troubles are all behind you. You've come to the right place. After a few sessions, your memory will be so clear, you'll remember everything, right back to the taste of your first tears, as you left your mother's womb!'

All I had to do with Ngampika was drink what he gave me while he went through a few chants for the spirits. According to him, their role was to inscribe in huge letters everything that had been wiped from my memory and to supply me with millions more blank pages on which to write my present and my future in capital letters. He gave me cricket's piss to drink, and green mamba blood, toad's spit, elephant hair mixed with kaolin and sparrow turds. Ngampika treated me like one of his family, inviting me to share his midday meal before the start of each consultation.

'Do the white doctors know you have to get someone to eat before you can treat them? I've had sick people here who weren't actually sick at all, they were just hungry, and you should have seen them eat! Like you!'

It was almost as though I was going to Ngampika's place just for the food. I could be sure of a generous lunch, lovingly prepared by his wife, a toothless old woman who disappeared immediately after placing two big aluminium bowls before us. I'd lift the lid, find my pieces of meat in peanut sauce, and manioc balls, which I devoured rapidly, because she really knew how to cook. I don't know what she put in her food, but I couldn't stop, and she had to give me two helpings. And if the pot was empty, Ngampika, who nibbled rather than ate, gave me what was left in his plate.

I ate many things at the healer's house, but my favourite was the antelope dish. The aroma of peanut sauce, mixed with strong spices and the smell of pepper, drove me wild. I swallowed the pieces of manioc and meatballs without chewing them, and the pepper prickled my guts. Then I'd lick my plate to show my hosts that my belly still wasn't full. And when I got diarrhoea for a few days, Ngampika wasn't concerned:

'It's to be expected, it's all the bad things hidden in your brain coming out at last!'

'Why are they coming out the far end?'

'Where did you think they'd come out?'

'Through my mouth...'

'Oh no, in traditional healing, all the diseases of the upper parts, that's to say, of the head, come out the bottom end, and all the lower diseases come out the top end. Your cure is underway, Little Pepper!'

One evening, after several glasses of palm wine, Ngampika suggested I spend the night at his place.

'My masks need to watch you sleep. While you're asleep they can enter your head and remove the impurities that stop your memory working properly.'

His wife laid out a mat for me in the living room with a sheet, all covered in blood stains. Seeing me look at the sheet in disgust, Ngampika said:

'We have washed the sheet, but blood doesn't come out easily! It's nothing to worry about...'

The one hurricane lamp in the house had been extinguished, and it felt as though the eyes of the masks were turned on me like torches. Ngampika and his wife were snoring away in the only bedroom. Curiously, the snores seemed to be coming from the masks. As luck would have it, I eventually managed to doze off. But at once, in my dream, I found myself pursued by an army of masks, cackling and pointing spears at me. I ran faster than them, as swiftly and easily as you'd expect of a man wearing seven league boots. I leaped over lakes, jumped across rivers, sometimes took off into the air on the edge of a forest and landed at the top of a tree to take a few minutes' rest, proud to have shaken off my pursuers. Then, to my despair, I heard them less than five hundred metres away. As I plunged onwards with gritted teeth and fists clenched, they went down other, darker paths, through tangled bush, dense forest, infested with mosquitoes, green mambas and ravenous boas. I heard the poor masks screaming in pain, probably from thorns and insect bites.

This hectic chase came to an end at the first cock crow and when I mercifully woke to find day breaking and the masks restored to their places on the wall, sulking because I'd won out against them, I knew Ngampika would have difficulty curing me...

As I wasn't getting better, Ngampika couldn't be paid. He was huffy with me now, and we sat looking at each other like china dogs. He no longer railed against Dr Lucien Kilahou or boasted of his roots going back through the kingdoms of Congo, via Angola and Cameroon.

'No food here today,' he announced one day, as he stood in the doorway.

'You should have warned me! I haven't eaten since this morning, I thought I was going to eat here as usual!'

He flared up at the cheek of my response:

'As usual? Oh that's great! Food costs money! Do you think we pick it up off the floor of the Grand Marché? Cricket's piss, mamba blood, toad's spit, elephant hair mixed with kaolin and sparrow's turds, it all costs a fortune! I've made two trips to Cameroon to get them! And who paid my travel expenses? Shall I tell you what my masks say about you among themselves? They think you're faking your illness to get out of paying! They tested you out when you spent the night here and they're quite blunt about it: you're the biggest imposter in this whole town, in the whole country, even! You can't fool me! If you don't proceed to check out right now I'll be checking you out with a one-way ticket to the next world!'

After a period of mature reflection, I returned to Ngampika's the following day with some cricket's piss, mamba blood, toad spit, elephant hair mixed with kaolin and sparrow turds. My neighbour, who knew about the healer's change of mood, had helped me prepare a dish of porcupine and spinach. But when Ngampika saw the basket full of food, he roared:

'Don't you dare set foot in my house today! The wrath of the masks is upon you!'

'Look, I've brought some food, we can eat together, your wife can join us.'

The old lady must have been listening to us in secret. She rose up behind him and yelled in her quavering voice:

'Profiteer! My husband cured you of malnutrition, you must pay us! Repay us for the food you ate! It was me that prepared it, I'm not your slave!'

She vanished as quickly as she'd appeared, and Ngampika took up her words:

'You heard what she said didn't you? You're healed, you have to pay us!'

'I'm not healed, and I won't pay! Did I ever ask your wife to bring me food to eat?'

'Then get out of here and go and see some other sucker, or go back and see Dr Lucien Kilahou, Ngampika is an honourable man, and does not wish to deal with a huckster like you!'

'I'm a huckster?'

'Yes, you are! A huckster and a scrounger!'

'And you're a criminal! You've never actually cured anyone! Your wife is a sorceress, she made my illness worse with her food!'

'Are you talking about my wife? You better watch out, weirdo! Ten curses be upon you! You'll see what happens to you, this is just the start of your problems!'

I left with my food, because Ngampika threatened to send dangerous animals after me in my sleep. I'd be surrounded by creatures with animal heads and human bodies. And the animal men, he predicted, would fire their poison darts into my brains. I don't know where he got these ideas from…

I had disappointed my neighbour, who had bust his guts for the sake of my health. His little lecture seemed almost to suggest he was giving up on me:

'Little Pepper, it can't always be you who's right, and the others – Dr Kilahou, Ngampika – who are wrong.'

Basically he was right, and it was up to me now to take the situation in both hands.

In any case, I had nothing left to lose.

The Moroccan

'D HAD A GREEN OUTFIT made up by a tailor in the Three Hundreds, who was used to this kind of commission. I wore long, pointed shoes that I'd picked up from the West Africans in the Grand Marché, in the medieval style. My hood, which was also green, was topped with a peacock feather which I'd plucked from the great bird that strutted up and down strangely outside my shack, as though he'd been sent by evil spirits or ill-intentioned people, to discover what was happening in my head.

No, I didn't ride on horseback, and I didn't have a bow like Robin Hood. I'd walked at a fairly rapid pace for half an hour along the banks of the Tchinouka, with a knife in my left hand, muttering over and over to myself that Moses was forty, the age I was then, when, appalled by the day-to-day wretchedness of his people, he killed an Egyptian foreman who was attacking an Israelite…

As the sun's rays glanced off the blade of my knife, I had the feeling my memory was coming back at last, and that this weapon would help me recover my identity, and free me from the chains of ill fortune I'd inherited from the father I was never going to meet.

The very fact of having a knife in my hands certainly proved I was a Bembé, who are skilled in handling a knife, just as Robin Hood was with his bow…

Was I strong enough to become the Robin Hood of Pointe-Noire, or would I remain forever, in the minds of my bandit contemporaries, the boy whose most remarkable feat was first to have sprinkled pepper powder in the food of the twins, Songi-Songi and Tala-Tala, and then become their sidekick? It was not enough to win me my place in posterity. I reckoned I was worth more, I just had to prove it...

*

I had bought the knife in the late morning from the boutique of a Moroccan, Ahmed XVI, near the Kassai roundabout. Despite the confusion clouding my mind, for the first time I experienced the pleasure of memories resurfacing, even if they were still somewhat sporadic. Something was happening inside me, and I even remembered it was the Moroccan tradesman who had helped me choose a knife, standing behind me like a shadow at five past midday, for fear I'd leave the bazaar empty-handed.

'Come on comrade, why hesitate? You're a good guy, we'll agree a price, we're like family! Sure you don't want a shot gun? I've got two that could wipe out an elephant...'

'No, I want a knife.'

'Well you won't be disappointed with that one! I, Ahmed XVI, son of Ahmed XV, grandson of Ahmed XIV, great-grandson of Ahmed XIII and so on and so forth, will make you a bargain, because you're an African brother, we've got the same blood, and thanks to your country I can feed my family, and send a bit of money to my brothers and cousins who still live back in my native village, in the south-west of Morocco, in Merzouga. Back there, as children, we learned to play among the dunes, to play hide and seek in the Sahelian desert and scrounge a few coins from the tourists doing their camel treks or bivouacking just a kilometre from our village!'

He was all set to tell me his life story. To stem the flow, I stroked the blade of the knife, and then the handle.

His shopkeeper's eyes gleamed:

'It's yours comrade! This knife is yours! I swear on my mother's life I'll earn nothing from it, but what matters is to serve a brother in need. It's made of stainless steel, it's actually a Victorinox, a highly regarded Swiss brand... Look at the blade, it can slice through air! And look at the handle. What a beauty! You have a good eye, my fellow African!'

Deep down I couldn't give a damn about his sales patter, for which he was known as one of the shiftiest shopkeepers in Pointe-Noire, so some people wouldn't even set foot in his shop, because even if you said you had no money, he'd reply:

'Who mentioned money? Does Ahmed XVI run this business for personal profit?'

He would give you the goods on credit, confident that you'd be back in his shop again one day.

Gossip had it that the Moroccan had brought his sorcery with him from North Africa and that outside his boutique was a mirror which, when you looked in it, cast a spell on you and got you to buy any old rubbish. And the mirror had to be 'fed'. Put plainly, the Moroccan sacrificed a client every six months to make the mirror work, resulting in two traffic accidents a year outside his shop, which stood on a major crossroads where vehicles came from all four corners of the town and got caught in endless traffic jams. Although the shopkeeper was held to be to blame for the accidents, no one dared hold him to account, since they were scared he'd retaliate and send the head of anyone speaking ill of him all the way back to Morocco. In Pointe-Noire, when someone said your head would get 'sent to Morocco' it meant you were going to die. The Pontenegrins were actually referring to the food tins marked *Made in Morocco*, in which the sardines were always headless. What did the Moroccans do with these heads? No one would ever know, and Ahmed played on the people's fear to frighten his detractors:

'If you keep bothering me and spreading lies about me, I'll send your heads to Morocco!'

I didn't want to have my head sent to Morocco either, so I didn't bother arguing with Ahmed XVI. I just wanted to get out of his shop with a knife, stainless steel or not.

'Does this knife cut well?' I asked him.

He gave me a long, hard look:

'Brother, that depends what kind of meat you want to cut! I can assure you, you won't be disappointed with its twenty-five centimetre stainless steel blade...'

I tossed two ten thousand CFA franc notes onto his counter.

The shopkeeper looked annoyed:

'No, my fellow African! Why are you giving me that now? Go and use your knife, and if you're satisfied with it, come and pay me... Can I just ask, why are you dressed like that, all in green with a feather on your head?'

I was already out of his shop, heading for the Tchinouka...

✳

The river Tchinouka divides Pointe-Noire in two, diving into the darkest recesses of the town, dallying for several kilometres in the Rex and Saint-Francois districts, looping round the Mongo-

Kamba cemetery, as though out of respect for the sleep of the dead, before vomiting into the sea all the impurities the Pontenegrins throw into its belly.

The river is known to be more dangerous than the Atlantic Ocean. In times of heavy rain its temper rises, and it swallows up solidly built houses, overturns the huge lorries of the Pointe-Noire transport company and renders most of the major highways impassable, so that people stay in their houses for a week, or longer.

I have lost count of how many times I walked up and down the right bank before finding at last the little bridge that leads to the Vongou district, the place where I believed I would at last become happy like other men again, but knowing also that I must commit the final act, driving out the spirits that were lodged in my body, corrupting my memory, the spirits I must cast once and for all into the depths of the Tchinouka, to be swept out into the Atlantic, where Nzinga, great ancestor, would destroy them for ever…

*

The people I passed in the street first stepped out of my way, then turned on their heels and ran when they saw I had a knife and that my dress was out of keeping with the present day.

I was proud to see that I could terrify people with a simple object everyone has in their home, as Dr Lucien Kilahou would have said. Some of them threw themselves into the river when I slashed at the air with my knife to frighten them even more.

As the day began to fade, I plunged on ahead with my eyes fixed on a large, brightly lit building. I adjusted my peacock feather, which each gust of wind almost blew off my hood. Tight in my hand I gripped the knife, which soon was to restore my lost dignity. I was only a few hundred metres from the sumptuous dwelling, with a wall twice as thick as my waist, guarded by two men standing straight as electric pylons.

A memory of the orphanage at Loango crossed my mind, and I thought for a moment that the two guards were Old Koukouba and Little Vimba.

Yes, I was only a few hundred metres from the house, when I noticed a black car with smoked glass windows draw up outside the entrance. One of the guards rushed to open the driver's door and at long last I saw up close the man who'd taken Maman Fiat 500 from me. It had always been his way, to show the Pontenegrins he drove his own car, and didn't need bodyguards, but had been obliged to accept the two guards outside his house for the security of his family, and besides they were only armed with truncheons. But his demagogy would not be enough for him this evening, for I was about to gather all my strength and throw myself upon the very person I detested most in all the world, more even than Dieudonné Ngoulmoumako.

Loango

T WAS SAID DURING my trial that I acted under the influence of insanity, and I'm banned from ever picking up a knife, now, even a plastic one.

Apparently the place where I'm imprisoned today is the site of the orphanage where I spent the first thirteen years of my life. The old buildings have been destroyed, replaced by those of this new penitentiary centre for criminals deemed to be 'not responsible for their actions'.

I'm allowed to write, to fill page after endless page, the whole day long. At least someone's keeping an eye on me, and the Director, Rémi Kata Likambo, often says I won't be able to kill anyone with a pencil.

On Sundays I go with my fellow detainees to a prayer room, where a Zairian pastor talks to us about God. When he found out my birth name was *Tokumisa Nzambe po Mose yamoyindo abotami namboka ya Bakoko* he sent out an instruction that it should never be used. But nor did he want me to be called simply 'Moses', though privately I believe I deserve this name because I liberated the people of Pointe-Noire from François Makélé, that maggot of a mayor who cared nothing about the living conditions of the Pontenegrins, and had probably got rid of Maman Fiat 500 and her girls in the Diosso Gorges. It was there they discovered a mass grave where most of the victims of his campaign 'Zero Zairian whores in Pointe-Noire' were heaped. The whole operation turned into a blood bath because of the hatred between our country and Zaire, fanned by politicians in the run up to elections.

It seems to me this priest, whose name I've forgotten, was a hypocrite. He's a tall man, who wears tailored suits that don't smell of mothballs – which is sufficient reason for me to hate him. Sometimes he gets in a muddle and speaks in English for a moment, just to show us he learned Holy Scripture in that language, which none of us understands. And he seems so distant and superior and looks at us disdainfully, as though he considers us a lost cause, unworthy of redemption…

I really must not forget to mention that I have a friend I get on well with, to whom I gave these confessions to read, having begun them several months ago, while I was being detained at Mbulamatadi, before being transferred here only a week after the works were finished – which is why everything round here is spanking new.

My friend kept my script for ten days, and during that time he avoided me in the canteen, the refectory and communal showers. I was unhappy with this, because I wanted to impress him, to show him I wasn't just a vegetable or vulgar criminal. He gave me back my pages, saying that when he had time himself – as if he didn't have plenty here – he would write down his story, which he wants to tell no one, not even me.

His name is Ndeko Nayoyakala, and he's about forty years old, like me. Though his face is gaunt and wasted, his Herculean build stops anyone from picking a fight. He has problems with his brain, as well, and as soon as he gave me back my manuscript I flicked through it while he stood there and saw that he'd been unable to resist correcting a misspelling here, an anachronism there. We quarrelled over a tiny little comma that he said was in the wrong place, and which I wanted to keep just where it was.

Ever since I found him here, Ndeko Nayoyakala has kept to the same routine: in the morning he stands by the window in his cell and draws the passing planes.

One day I'd had enough of his obsession with flying machines, and talked to him about my childhood friend, and how he'd had the same passion too.

He looked at me for a moment:

'What was his name?'

'Bonaventure...'

'Bonaventure who?'

'Bonaventure Kokolo...'

He stood there, deep in thought, for a few seconds, then murmured, without looking up:

'I'll keep on drawing planes till the day I see a real one come and land outside the asylum, to take me away from here...'

About the Author

Alain Mabanckou was born in Congo in 1966. An award-winning novelist, poet, and essayist, Mabanckou currently lives in Los Angeles, where he teaches literature at UCLA. He is the author of *African Psycho, Broken Glass, Black Bazaar*, and *Tomorrow I'll Be Twenty*, as well as *The Lights of Pointe-Noire* (The New Press). In 2015, Mabanckou was a finalist for the Man Booker International Prize.

About the Translator

Helen Stevenson is a piano teacher, writer, and translator who lives in Somerset, England. Her translation of Mabanckou's *The Lights of Pointe-Noire* won the Grand Prix, 2015 French Voices Award.

Celebrating 25 Years of Independent Publishing

Thank you for reading this book published by The New Press. The New Press is a nonprofit, public interest publisher celebrating its twenty-fifth anniversary in 2017. New Press books and authors play a crucial role in sparking conversations about the key political and social issues of our day.

We hope you enjoyed this book and that you will stay in touch with The New Press. Here are a few ways to stay up to date with our books, events, and the issues we cover:

- Sign up at www.thenewpress.com/subscribe to receive updates on New Press authors and issues and to be notified about local events
- Like us on Facebook: www.facebook.com/newpress books
- Follow us on Twitter: www.twitter.com/thenewpress

Please consider buying New Press books for yourself; for friends and family; and to donate to schools, libraries, community centers, prison libraries, and other organizations involved with the issues our authors write about.

The New Press is a 501(c)(3) nonprofit organization. You can also support our work with a tax-deductible gift by visiting www.thenewpress.com/donate.